Joann

Book Five in the Apron Strings Series

OTHER BOOKS IN THE SERIES

Polly by Naomi Musch

Nellie by Amy Walsh

Priscilla by Jenny Knipfer

Beatrice by Patti Wolf

Cynthia by Jessica Marie Holt

Renee by Sandra Ardoin

Cassie by Lisa R. Howeler

Kristen by Dawn Klinge

Paige by Regina Walker

Maddie by Dawn Kinzer

Aileron Books

donnajostone.com

Copyright ©2024 by Donna Jo Stone

Published in the United States of America
Publication Date May 2024

Cover Design and Formatting by Samantha Fury

More by Donna Jo Stone

A Wedding to Remember

(A Bed & Breakfast Novelette)

Coming 2024

When the Wildflowers Bloom Again

(Historical Southern Fiction)

Promise Me Tomorrow

(YA Contemporary)

INTRODUCTION

From *Mrs. Canfield's Cookery Book*

Dear Friends,

How glad I am that this cookery book has made its way into your hands. I hope it will become more than a collection of recipes, and that in your home it will help foster an environment filled with love, family, friends, and of course, good food. Cooking and baking are more than necessary skills for a homemaker. They can be an art form. They can be a ministry. Most of all they can be a way to show love.

Food is an essential and everyday part of our lives, but it can be so much more. I hope through the pages of this book you will find not only instruction but also inspiration for your body and your soul.

Happy cooking and baking! May you give and receive many blessings through your efforts.

Warmly,
Mrs. Clara Canfield

CHAPTER ONE

Joann's dad was so unreasonable.

He acted like she was a child, not a grown woman of twenty-four who'd been working in the family store since she was fourteen.

With her back to her father, Joann jerked a Spiderman comic from the rack and realigned it with the others. Her shoulder-length ginger hair fell forward. She shoved it back. No doubt her bouffant had flattened to her skull and her eyeliner had smudged during the long day. She wasn't vain, by any account, but would feel more collected and ready to stand her ground if she didn't resemble a disheveled raccoon.

It would be better to take up the fight another time, but she couldn't hold her tongue. "All I said was we might update the store if we added 45s of pop music to the shelves." Anything by the Beatles would sell out in a day.

"And why would I do that?" His chin puckered in a scowl as he scratched the fringe of gray hair at the back of his head.

Howard Kincaid was a short, compact bulldog of a man, all bark. Everyone knew he adored Joann and her sister, but he was as stubborn as they came.

She said, "We carry everything else. Why not 45s?"

The lone store for miles, Kincaid's Mercantile stocked groceries, tools, toys, and even a smattering of clothing. What harm could come from Dad giving her a corner? They had room in the large, two-story building. From the road, it resembled an oversized white barn, but the interior rivaled any good-sized general store and grocery, with an upstairs to boot. Plenty of unused corners.

Dad shook his head. "No. I need to think of my customers."

"That's what I'm doing!"

She knew their customers. Many times over the years, Joann had practically run the store for weeks on end when Dad had suffered bouts of melancholy. During those times, she'd always kept the store open, stocked, and in the black.

Joann crossed her arms. "You act like I want to burn the place down. Adding to our stock will bring in business, not hurt it."

She shot a glance toward Barb, her younger-by-one-year sister, and hoped Barb caught her silent plea for support. Before broaching the subject of adding a new section to the store, Joann had set Barb to work nearby instead of upstairs among the stacks of overalls, household supplies, and tools.

Barb didn't seem to notice Joann's predicament, even though the whole topic of records had been Barb's idea in the beginning. Instead of engaging in the conversation, she crouched near the bottom shelf, listlessly arranging boxes of crackers. All hunched over and hiding behind her honey-colored hair, she could've been her high school self instead of a young woman who'd taken business classes for almost a year.

Joann cleared her throat. "Right, Barb?"

Blinking, Barb finally looked up, her fingers toying with the silver locket pendant at her throat. "Oh. Yes." Letting go of the pendant and dusting her hands on her beige shopkeeper's apron, she said, "Records are the new thing, Dad."

Great. Her sister had managed to find the exact wrong thing to say.

Dad shook his head and opened his mouth. Joann braced for another refusal, but the bell over the door tinkled, abruptly cutting off the conversation like the twist of a faucet.

Who came into a store five minutes before closing? Their hours were posted on the door.

Cora Lee wore pink stretch pants and had her hair covered with a green scarf. Hesitating on the welcome mat inside the door, she tipped her head to the side. Cora Lee was Joann's age and married. Now that her cheerleading days were over, she spent her time rooting out gossip. She didn't yet have a baby to keep her occupied.

Joann put on a bright, customer-service smile, though she made a show of examining her Timex. "Hey, Cora Lee. Can I help you find something?" She resisted the urge to straighten her own hair.

Cora Lee narrowed her eyes, a feline sniffing the air in search of a morsel to chew. "Nope. I'll only be a minute."

She wandered over to the cracker aisle where Barb was. After a few minutes of chatting, which Barb did not encourage, thank goodness, Cora Lee took the hint and went about her shopping.

Joann strode around the floor of the store, picking up stray cans of tuna and corn, first aid cream, and other items shoppers had displaced, returning them to the shelves. When Cora Lee finally approached the front, Joann slipped behind the counter, ready to check out the items.

Cora Lee placed half a dozen Granny Smiths, a can of baking powder, and a bottle of pink dish soap by the register. She gazed around the store as if she'd never seen the rows of foodstuffs, medicines, and stationery.

"Joann, you're so industrious! I could never do this job." She wrinkled her nose and smiled, an expression she probably practiced in the mirror. "Before I forget, I need to make sure you're still planning to color eggs for the Easter egg hunt. It's only three weeks away!"

"I am. Eight dozen, like always."

The store had been donating to the town's Easter egg hunt since long before Cora Lee got her first tooth, and Joann had colored eggs for the event every year since she turned ten. It wasn't likely she'd forget.

Joann tallied up Cora Lee's items and bagged them.

Four feet away, Dad stood pretending to sort seed packets, his presence letting her know the earlier conversation wasn't through yet. If he'd finished saying his piece about selling records, he'd have busied himself with one of the endless tasks always demanding the attention of a storekeeper.

Torn between giving him a few more minutes to cool off and the urge to get Cora Lee out the door, Joann found herself slowing the transaction.

She tapped the small box by the register. "Feel free to check the coupons. You might find one you need."

"Thanks." Cora Lee riffled through the stack, then shook her head. "Nothing here for me." The scarf covering her hair slipped, revealing oversized curlers.

"That's a shame." As Joann counted the change, she chirruped, "Have a nice evening!"

No doubt Cora Lee would be dressed and coifed with a hot meal on the table for her husband by the time he got home.

Joann couldn't imagine getting dolled up for an evening in.

The bell over the door tinkled, signaling Cora Lee's departure.

Imagining a book balanced on her head, Joann stretched her neck. Confidence was key. She admonished herself to stand up straight and planted her feet on the wood plank floor. "I wish you'd reconsider, Dad. Can't we even talk about it?"

Without taking a second to think over what she'd said, he replied, "Let me worry about what we carry in the store. I've done pretty good so far."

In the quiet, the old building settled, as if sighing in weariness at their argument.

The cash register remained open, and she slid the drawer forward into the machine. It didn't quite shut all the way, and she pulled the drawer out and tried again. This time, the mechanism allowed it to find home.

Her shoulders had rounded again, and she jerked them back. "There's nothing wrong with updating. Besides, you play music all the time. The customers like it."

"Playing a radio isn't the same as selling music," he grumbled. "Chasing fads is never a good business move." He ambled over to the large front window facing the street and flipped the open sign to closed.

"It's not a fad." Joann crossed her arms and slumped, unable to voice her true feelings.

It wasn't about records or music. It was about having her ideas considered. It was about respect.

She wasn't a child.

They needed to finish closing down the store. She retrieved the cash bag from under the counter and reopened the fidgety register. Why had she bothered fooling with the cantankerous equipment earlier instead of leaving it open? Habit. Doing things the right way. Putting up with worn out antiques to please her father.

She cleared the register of cash and the two checks they'd gotten since the day's bank run, before giving the drawer a hard shove, ignoring the way it sprang back open.

Her dad shot her a surprised look, followed by a pileup of worry lines across his forehead, but Joann pretended not to see.

Fuming, she walked the moneybag to the office in the back of the store and put it in the safe.

She stared at the office walls. Until she got under control, she didn't want to face anyone.

A tentative tap on the doorframe got her attention, but she didn't move except to glance halfway over one shoulder.

"I'll go on to the house and leave you girls to it." The gravel in Dad's voice conveyed regret. "I'll put some soup on for supper."

A concession, Joann knew, and the closest he'd come to an out-and-out apology. Canned soup was the extent of her dad's cooking skill. It would be either tomato or cream of mushroom, a poor repertoire for a man who'd raised two daughters on his own since they were twelve and eleven.

He'd taught her to add milk to soup with precision, always guiding, always doing his best. They were alike in this, and it hurt her to be at odds with him, but she needed to be seen just as much as she needed to make him proud.

She sighed. "We'll be home soon." She didn't remind him to mark the inventory sheet if he took a can from the store, which he would. They had soup at home, but he wouldn't be aware of that and would take one off the shelf.

A stack of invoices on the desk made a handy excuse, and she began sorting them, even though she stood on the wrong side of the desk.

After a beat, he gave two light taps to the doorframe, a departing signal. The air shifted at his leaving and the tension dissipated. Their home, situated across the street, would give them space apart for a bit. They needed it.

In a few minutes, she finished the paperwork and went to find Barb. She hadn't gotten far stocking the aisle, but had at least moved on from the crackers and had removed the day's newspapers from the rack in preparation for the next editions.

"What gives, Barb?"

It came out snippy, but Barb deserved it, leaving her out to dry.

"What?" The chain of her necklace had been clamped in her mouth, and now the locket fell, landing on her chest.

"You didn't back me up. What's wrong with you?"

Instead of answering, Barb pressed her lips together, ducked her head, and touched the locket again. It was a gift from Charles, an airman she'd met at a church rally over in Shreveport.

It had his picture inside. Joann didn't approve. Barb and the young serviceman were the same age, but Barb had always been young for her years.

Her tone moderated, Joann said, "You're so distracted."

Barb picked up a copy of *The Pecan Ridge Gazette* and Joann took it from her, getting ink smudges on her fingers.

Ineffectively, Joann rubbed her hands on her apron, getting it dirty with newsprint as well. She frowned at the stains. "It's that guy."

A look of pure misery crossed Barb's pale face.

Joann dropped the newspaper onto the counter. "What's wrong?"

Going by Barb's downcast posture and her fascination with the locket, a sob session about the boyfriend might delay dinner. Joann's heart ached. Love never lasted long. If the couple had broken up, Joann would feed her sister ice cream and paint her toenails. She'd brought Barb through breakups before. Unless it wasn't a breakup.

Her heart spasmed.

Maybe Charles had gotten orders to go on a mission to Vietnam. This past month, in March, President Johnson implemented the air strikes of Operation Rolling Thunder. A few weeks later, American marine combat troops had landed on a South Vietnamese beach.

Joann hadn't asked much about Charles at all. He worked with radar, she thought, or maybe maps. She'd been blinded by disapproval, sure the couple was a mismatch, destined for heartbreak. With a start, she realized, if she were being honest, she'd formed an opinion of the young man's involvement with Barb simply because they didn't know him well, or know his family.

She hadn't been fair.

Hesitant, Joann asked, "Is he … going somewhere? He hasn't been deployed, has he?"

"No, no. Nothing like that." Barb shook her head. "My stomach's been off, is all."

As soon as Barb mentioned it, Joann understood she'd misinterpreted her sister's listlessness, chalking it up to a normal lazy mood. Maybe those frequent trips to the bathroom weren't only from the soda she'd sipped all day.

"Why didn't you tell me you were ill?" Joann scolded, pressing the back of her hand to Barb's forehead. "Your eyes are overbright."

Barb shrugged her away. "It'll pass."

"Okay. Don't fuss." Hands up, Joann took a step back.

Barb shot her a dark look, which relieved rather than annoyed her. At least her sister was acting more normal.

Trying for a teasing jab to lighten the mood, Joann asked, "Are you sure it's not your boyfriend?"

Instead of a smile, serious lines took over Barb's face. She shook her head. "No. Nothing's wrong with Charles." The necklace went back into her mouth, a sign she wasn't telling the whole truth, but Joann let it go. For certain, Barb worried about Charles being sent overseas. How could she not?

Joann thought of Matty Delarue. He was stationed stateside, but Mrs. Delarue worried all the same. Years ago, the Delarues had lost two young children in a house fire and Mrs. Delarue had become overprotective of Matty. Considering the way she hovered over her son, him enlisting in the Army must've sent her into a panic. At first, she came by often and kept her chin up, but Joann could tell it was hard going. Nowadays, Mrs. Delarue rarely came to the store and hadn't requested a delivery for over a week.

Joann determined she'd check on the woman that evening before heading home.

She took Barb's arm, steering her toward the table where the old-timers liked to play checkers and chat every morning. "Why don't you rest, and I'll finish up."

Without protest, Barb took a seat.

"I won't be long."

Working her way through the store, Joann made sure all was secure, turning off lights as she went. Every time she clicked a light off, she said a prayer for the safety of the military, and for a quick end to the conflict in Vietnam.

The next day, Joann put a plate of scrambled eggs in front of Dad as he sat at the kitchen table. The morning was dressed in misty gray, dawn not making an appearance yet. Joann rarely cooked a breakfast at home, instead depending on the coffee and honey buns at the store.

"Dad?" Joann sat in the chair opposite him. "I need to talk to you about something."

"I don't want to hear anything about records, Joann. I said what I said." He shoveled eggs into his mouth as if it excused him from conversation.

"No, not that." Joann plowed ahead. "I went by Mrs. Delarue's yesterday."

His manner changed from rigid to concern. He paused midbite, put his fork down, and wiped his mouth. "How's she doing?"

"I think she could be better. She misses Matty."

Their long-time customer had welcomed Joann. More than the dusty house and the stained housedress Mrs. Delarue wore, the woman's listlessness gave Joann cause for concern. Mrs. Delarue was a fastidious woman, sweeping her porch daily and often seen weeding her flowerbeds. Her neatness extended to Matty's upbringing. As a child he had been the rough-and-tumble sort, but had always arrived at church with water-slicked hair and a tucked-in shirt.

"I'm worried about her. Do you suppose we could find her a job at the store? I'd like to offer her something to occupy her time. A responsibility." Joann frowned. "She shot down my suggestion of the quilting club. Claimed there's too much gossip in that circle for her taste. But I can't sit by if there's something I can do for her."

Dad gazed thoughtfully at Joann. "You have a tender heart, Jo." He picked up his fork. "I wouldn't have it any other way."

"Should I ask her to work at the store an afternoon or two a week?"

Dad nodded, a slow affirmation. "Sounds like a good idea to me. We've been needing extra help anyway."

Joann and her dad locked horns on occasion, but they were of the same mind when it came to their family's place in the town. Kincaid's was more than a place to shop, and the Kincaids were more than merchants. They were rooted in place, steeped in a heritage of drawing strength from the community and giving strength back.

Joann got up and moved the frying pan from the stove into the sink. "I'll go by today and see if she's willing."

CHAPTER TWO

The Wednesday before Easter Sunday, Joann dragged a folding table through the back door of the store. Morning dew soaked the hem of her slacks as she carried it around the side and to the front, where she would set up a fresh fruit and vegetable display. On an outside bench near the store entrance, Charles and Barb sat close together in private conversation. Inside, Dad readied an area near the big window for the old men who came for their papers, coffee, and a checker game or two.

Charles sat with his lanky frame bent over his knees, his hat in his hands. He twisted it around and around. Joann couldn't get a good look at his face, only the top of his head, dark hair with white scalp showing through the military cut, but she could tell he was upset.

She hesitated. "Is everything all right?"

Barb gave her head a shake. "His best friend from high school has been in a car accident."

Propping the folded table against the bench, Joann said, "I'm so sorry. In Wisconsin?"

Not making eye contact, Charles nodded and pinched the bridge of his nose. "They don't expect a good outcome."

An awkward pause ensued while Joann tightened the ties on her beige store apron. She never knew what to say in these situations. The desire to go fetch Charles a tissue or a blanket seized her.

As if blankets and tissues would help.

Barb tucked her arm into Charles's.

"I hope he gets well soon," Joann offered.

He nodded, trying on a smile, but his eyes remained clouded. A best friend in intensive care over nine hundred miles away was enough to upset anyone. He leaned into Barb.

Her little sister, Barb, suddenly a grown woman capable of comforting a grown man.

The foreign idea struck her as if she were observing a stranger, leaving her uneasy. Joann shook off the feeling, telling herself the sadness of the tragedy had affected her mind. Barb was the person she'd always been.

In the distance, a truck backfired, and the driver gunned it. The noise of Nathan's green farm truck announced his arrival long before it came into view. He'd never give up Ol' Bessie, as he called her. Joann smiled to herself.

When Nathan had gone off to college for three years, his father had leased out most of the farmland. One day Nathan planned to reclaim it all, but for now, he tended a small orchard and strawberry fields, along with a few honeybee hives. He even had two dozen evergreen trees and talked about planting more Christmas trees someday. Until then, Nathan kept busy. As a favor to her, every week he drove around to local farms picking up produce for those who didn't grow enough to bother making a trip into town themselves. He'd bring it to the store. The farms got to sell to her, and she got the choicest fresh produce the local region could provide. It worked out beautifully.

It didn't hurt that she got to see Nathan too.

The truck came to a shuddering stop right in front of the store, belching a plume of exhaust. Nathan cut the engine and gave a wave from the open window. She returned the gesture and hurried to set the table up. The sight of his ruddy face and friendly, gap-toothed smile warmed Joann to the tips of her toes, and it didn't seem right to feel so good, with Charles so down.

It was a shame Charles couldn't get leave to go see his friend. Wisconsin was a long way off.

On impulse, she turned to Charles and said, "Come to Sunday dinner next week. It's Easter."

Barb brightened and sat up straighter. "What a wonderful idea!" Out of Charles's line of vision, she mouthed a thank-you to Joann. Then she grabbed his hand. "Come early for church."

Joann left the two talking, walked over to the truck, and propped her elbows on Nathan's window. "Hey."

He winked. "What's shaking?"

Joann winked right back. "Your truck, looks like. But only when it's running."

He groaned. "You got me."

"Did you bring strawberries today?"

Nathan hopped out, and they walked around the truck to the tailgate. "These are my first batch." He picked up a flat and held them out.

Strawberries were her favorite. Possibly the reason he'd started planting them.

For three seasons during her teen years, Joann had helped at the Poole's orchard, a distraction from the empty house after her mother left and Dad had packed Barb off to church camp to learn music. A thirteen-year-old Nathan had teased her, saying she ate more than she picked. He'd acted normal around her. She'd needed normal. Then Mrs. Poole passed away from ovarian cancer, and Joann and Nathan had bonded through unbearable sorrows punctuated with occasional childish spats.

He knew her so well it both pleased and spooked her.

Joann inhaled, her mouth watering at the heady scent. "I hope I can keep from eating the profits." She popped a berry into her mouth and sweetness exploded across her tongue. "These are wonderful." She reached for a crate. "Once we're unloaded, help yourself to coffee inside. Fresh brewed."

"Anything for coffee." He took the strawberries from her and placed them beside the display she'd set up.

"I'll help." Charles handed his hat to Barb.

Dad ambled out of the shop and onto the front porch area. "Why are you kids unloading in front instead of around back?" He propped his hands on his hips, a lord surveying his property.

Charles had gotten to his feet, but now stood awkwardly glancing from person to person.

As if she hadn't heard Dad, Joann concentrated on arranging vegetables. Nathan, out of earshot or choosing to pretend to be, stacked several crates in the truck bed. Casually inching closer to the truck, Charles did a good job acting natural. No doubt dealing with drill sergeants taught him to keep a blank face.

From the corner of her eye, Joann cast a sideways glance at her dad. She took a marker and price cards from her front pocket. "Faster to unload the first batch this way." She wrote on the cards and stuck them in the proper places. "Nathan will bring the rest to the loading area in a minute."

Huffing, Dad shuffled back inside, leaving a suddenly nervous Charles clutching a bushel basket of green-topped beets.

"Let me," Barb said. She began putting them into one of the crates on the display table.

Arms straining, Nathan carried a stack of three boxes over and set them down.

Joann said, "I think we have enough for the front. Can you take the rest to the rear entrance?"

This earned her the response of an affirmative grunt. Sometimes she wished he would talk more, but that was the way of men.

In response to him, Joann gave an abbreviated wave. "I'll be there to help in a minute."

The lovebirds shuffled vegetables around, not really doing anything besides standing close to each other. Barb didn't seem to mind him crowding her.

The uneasy feeling returned, but Joann batted it away as if it were a pesky fly.

Barb deserved happiness, but she wouldn't latch onto Charles. Even if the world settled, a military wife must go wherever Uncle Sam willed. Barb had never been the adventurous type. She'd never want to leave the store. The girls had always planned on running it together.

Two ladies carrying canvas shopping totes appeared on the street and headed toward the store. They were like birds coming out of nowhere for breadcrumbs.

Joann greeted them by name before saying, "Fresh for you, ladies! I'll meet you inside to ring you up."

Nathan cranked the truck, and this time didn't gun it, but eased into the track along the side of the building, barely disturbing the skittish mama cat sitting in a spot of sun at the corner of the store. Nathan's gentleness with small creatures always made Joann misty-eyed.

Straightening her hair and apron as she walked along, Joann chose to slip around the side of the building rather than walk through and risk getting into a conversation with her father. Strawberry stains covered her palms, and she wiped her hands on her apron, but stickiness remained. Were her lips stained as well? Lips made her think of kissing, and kissing made her think of Nathan, and she blushed hot. The store was no place to entertain silly, romantic notions. For a time, she'd harbored girlish dreams. They'd always been close, but after their tumultuous teen years, the relationship had settled, landing somewhere between friendship and romance. He'd wanted it that way and she'd agreed, eventually. An occasional friendly date with Nathan, no strings attached, would have to suit. Besides, everyone knew heavy romance led to marriage, and marriage would blow any plans Joann had for the store out of the water. She had to be sensible.

Maybe someday things would be different, but for now, neither of them was in a hurry to jump into a more serious relationship.

By the time she approached the open back door, only a few bushels of produce remained in the truck bed. Male conversation and laughter drifted from the interior of the storeroom. If Dad had caught Nathan, they'd talk for a good while. Joann hadn't inherited her dad's gift of gab and flair. Practical and hardworking, she approached store work differently, but they both loved the old place.

Joann hefted one of the last crates, breaking a nail in the process. She groaned. She'd just gotten them all even. Such was the life of a shopkeeper. As she approached the back door, Nathan emerged.

"Let me get that." He took the crate from her.

"I had it."

"I know."

The burden had been heavier than she'd estimated, too heavy for her, really, something she'd never admit. Although she had to admit one thing, he had the muscle for the job. Against her will, her gaze lingered on his shoulders.

He turned around and she lowered her lashes, concentrating on her broken nail.

Nathan cleared his throat. "So, Barb's beau is invited to Easter dinner?"

"He is." Joann bent to unload carrots, letting her hair fall forward and hide her over-warm face. "You can come if you want. And your dad, of course."

"Of course." Nathan tried to smother his grin. "Dad will appreciate a nice, home-cooked meal."

"Will he come to church before?"

"That would be pushing it, but I'll make the invitation from you instead of me. Who knows? He might show up."

"Does he have a suit?"

"A suit!" Nathan staggered back in mock horror. "Who said anything about dressing up?" He slumped dramatically. "I suppose you'll want us to bathe too."

"Oh, you."

She swiped at his head with the fronds of a carrot bunch, and he ducked away, laughing.

Laughing along with him, she said, "Go unload the rest of the produce."

Joann filled a small box with medium-sized strawberries and put it aside for the family's use later, a perk of owning a store. Dad always said if you had peace and plenty, you were well-blessed.

Plenty surrounded them.

But with the state of the world, peace was a bit harder to come by these days.

***

The bell at the entrance of the store chimed a constant greeting to customers as they bustled in. Joann's stomach rumbled. She'd let all the others take lunch first, meaning to go last, but it had gotten busy and she'd missed her chance. The morning strawberries she'd sampled were nothing but a memory. Smiling at the last customer, she handed over change. "You have a Happy Easter."

It was a blessing Mrs. Delarue had come to help them out, since their regular daytime help had called in with tonsillitis.

Mrs. Delarue hurried to open the door for the customer. Wavy, shoulder-length mahogany hair declared their new part-time employee had been to the hairdresser, and her blue-flowered dress was fresh and crisp beneath her store apron. The slight woman was subdued but pleasant and friendly enough, and closer to cheerful than she'd been when Joann had visited her at home. It did Joann's heart good to see the woman perking up. Thank goodness Mrs. Delarue's husband had approved of his wife working an afternoon here and there. A warm glow suffused Joann's spirit. In the end, all parties would benefit. Hopefully.

The older lady excelled at friendliness, but wasn't proficient on the register. Or stocking.

They'd work on it. After a day or two, Mrs. Delarue would gain confidence.

Customers trickled out and business slowed. Joann surveyed the store. Barb helped a young boy by reading his shopping list and retrieving a loaf of Sunbeam from the top shelf. Only one other customer browsed the aisles.

Time for Joann to grab a break while she could.

She tapped Barb on the shoulder. "Can you watch the register? Let Mrs. Delarue practice the next sale if she wants to." With a smile and a wave to the boy, Joann grabbed some cheese and crackers and headed to the back of the store.

In the back room, Dad stood near one of the shelves full of stock, running his finger along the labels and squinting at the print. "I didn't like Nathan's truck in front of the store."

Couldn't he give her a moment to relax before starting in again?

She said, "It was only there for a minute."

"Longer than a minute."

"But we were able to set up quicker and draw in customers," she pointed out.

"They would've come."

Or not. Mrs. Jacobs had stopped on her way to a doctor appointment, but Joann held her tongue, not willing to go ten rounds with her father when all she wanted was to rest her aching feet and eat her lunch. She sat down and bit into a cracker.

"I don't want you changing anything up without running it by me first."

Joann chewed.

"I mean it, Joann. This store is our family's heritage, and the name Kincaid means something in Pecan Ridge. People have expectations." He found the box he was looking for and retrieved a packet of nails.

He said, "See you up front."

Joann didn't get up until every last cracker was gone and she'd swept the last crumb from her apron.

On her way back into the main part of the store, she passed by the old photos on the wall, shots of the store through the ages and portraits of the founding Kincaids and their progeny, all the way to a picture of herself and Barb posing by the front window. She backed up to straighten a frame, staring into the eyes of Great-Grandma Lacey, her dad's grandmother, a woman who had led the family business, and the family, with a steady hand without the help of any man for thirty-nine years. Dad spoke of her with awe.

Joann sighed.

If only he could have a speck of the faith in Joann that he'd had in his grandmother.

All she wanted was a fair chance to prove she was worthy of the Kincaid name.

CHAPTER THREE

The store closed for Good Friday, and after morning services and lunch, the Kincaids returned home. Instead of going to his room or the den-turned-library where all the magazines Dad collected went to live, Dad preferred the living room. He reclined in his navy La-Z-Boy, an item Joann had talked him into buying for himself, and tented an old copy of Life over his face as he "rested his eyes." He'd nap, but the girls had a meal to prep for.

Even with a stool and as tall as she was, Joann had to stretch to reach the top cupboard over the Frigidaire. The roasting pan spent most of the year tucked away, but with Charles coming to dinner, *and* Nathan *and* his father—thanks to her big mouth—now she had a dinner to cook with only two days to prepare. Dad insisted they prepare one of the largest hams available since they would have company, but how much ham could six people eat? Days of leftovers and sandwiches loomed in the future. Good thing Dad wasn't picky.

"I'm so excited Charles is coming!" Barb said, as she took the pan from Joann and placed it on the white Formica countertop.

Joann stepped down from the stool and tucked it away between the fridge and the adjacent cabinet.

"I have something." Barb dug into her straw tote and retrieved a yellow-brown hardback book, handing it to Joann. "Charles can't cook a lick, but gave me this."

"What is it?" Joann gingerly examined the old book, reading the title, *Mrs. Canfield's Cookery Book.*

"It's his mother's."

A family heirloom? As if the book had scorched her, Joann quickly set it on the kitchen table. "His mother's?" She bit her tongue to keep from asking why on earth he would give them his mother's cookbook, of all things. It was the kind of thing a man gave to a girl he expected to be around for a while. Joann put her hand on her stomach and pressed against the hurt there. But why had he given the book to them?

As if she'd read Joann's mind, Barb volunteered, "I told him we didn't have a cookbook." She caught her bottom lip between her teeth. "But I didn't tell him why."

After mother left, Dad had purged the house of all her books, including cookbooks. Joann learned to cook from recipes she'd clipped from magazines or given to her by church ladies. Family favorites she taped inside the cabinet doors. The others found a home in the bottom kitchen drawer.

Barb slouched against the counter and ran her finger along the metal strip edging. "Charles said we could use the cookbook or not, but I thought it was super sweet of him." She giggled. Her mouth turned up at the corners, pleased, rather like the cat who got the cream. It was the same expression she wore any time someone gave her a little attention.

Joann relaxed.

Whatever had been troubling Barb over the last few weeks had apparently resolved itself. Just as Joann had suspected it would. Big sister always knew.

Barb took a seat at the table and leafed through the cookbook, taking care with the pages. "Look, Joann!" She rotated the book and pointed to the tiny print. "We could try this one out."

Squinting, Joann hunched over the book and read the title aloud. "St. Germaine Soup. Never heard of it." She straightened, pulled out the chair opposite her sister, and sat.

"And you say Dad never wants to try anything new." Barb scanned the recipe. "It's pea soup." She puckered her lips. "At least I think it is. Marrowfat peas are green peas, right?"

"Hmmm. I thought I'd make a gelatin mold with fresh strawberries. I saved some back."

Groaning, Barb rolled her eyes heavenward. "You always make a gelatin mold. If we can't do something different, can we at least have a coconut cake? It's Easter, for goodness' sake."

"But you don't like coconut."

"It's festive." Barb fiddled with the salt and pepper shakers. "Besides, it's Charles's favorite."

Joann cocked an eyebrow. "Are you taking up cooking to please a man now?"

Since the grilled cheese incident when Barb had left a burner on to answer the phone, Joann and her dad had teased Barb unmercifully about her cooking skills, or lack of.

Barb sniffed. "I've always wanted to learn to cook. Let me see if I can find the recipe." The frown creasing her forehead deepened as she examined the pages. "There isn't one here specifically for coconut cake, but I know he said his mother makes it all the time. It must be here." With a finger, she traced the columns. Finally, she paused. "Here's plain white cake, the closest I can find. And it has a check mark next to it. I guess she just adds frosting and coconut?"

She looked so serious, her expression asking for affirmation.

Joann fell into her big sister role. Nodding, she said, "You're probably right. Does he like cherries on it?"

"I don't know." Barb's eyes widened. Tiny specks of green in her light-brown irises caught the light, a color that only showed when high emotion contracted her pupils.

"Don't worry. We'll put the cherries to the side and ask him at dinner. They go on at the last minute anyway."

CHAPTER FOUR

Easter morning materialized as a drippy affair. Maybe it would clear up in time for the kids' afternoon Easter egg hunt in the town park. Holidays were meant for children, and Joann hated to think of their disappointment.

"Are you almost ready, Barb?" she yelled from the kitchen, busily pouring brown sugar glaze over the ham. A kerchief covered her poufy bouffant hair, and she'd tossed an old apron over her navy sheath dress. The table had already been set. The ham needed to go in before they left, or it would never be done in time. Hopefully, pastor's sermon wouldn't go long. No one liked dried out ham.

Not a murmur from Barb made its way to the kitchen. After Joann slid the ham into the oven, she checked her watch.

Barb had better not make them late.

Joann hurried to the bathroom door and gave it a sharp rap. "I need in there."

The door opened and a cloud of hairspray escaped into the hall, stinging Joann's eyes. She fanned away the fumes.

"Sorry." Barb squeezed by.

"Wow." Forgetting her earlier annoyance, Joann admired her sister's flipped up bob beneath a barely there pink hat. "You look beautiful."

With a white-gloved hand, Barb squeezed Joann's forearm. "Almost as pretty as my big sis. But you better hurry."

"I'm not the one holding up the show," Joann grumbled under her breath.

She took her turn at the mirror, finishing her hair and simple makeup of eyeliner, mascara, and coral lipstick. Next, she hastily arranged her hat on her hair. It was mostly netting sprinkled with half a dozen navy grosgrain bows the same color as her dress, shoes, and clutch purse.

The overall effect turned out less stylish than she'd imagined, and more funeral than Easter, but it would have to do.

At the door, she grabbed a tattered umbrella. Last one out couldn't be picky, she supposed.

By the time she locked the door, Dad's blue Deville was idling in the drive. She hurried out to the car and hopped in the back, since Barb had already taken the front seat, per usual.

Dad smiled over his shoulder. "There's my pretty girl." Facing front, he put the car in gear.

When they pulled into the church's gravel parking lot, Nathan and Mr. Poole stood waiting under the covered walkway with umbrellas worthy of Sunday service, unlike hers. She shoved the old umbrella under her seat.

Nathan headed over to meet them and opened Joann's door, shielding her from a light drizzle as she got out. These days with Nathan, she often felt delicate and protected. She liked it. Dangerous ground, she reminded herself, because she and Nathan had an understanding. She shouldn't get too attached. After all, hadn't he had a string of girlfriends at college? Not that she'd had any claim on him then. Not now, either.

Besides, she was supposed to be an independent woman, capable of running the store, not a swooning female.

Keep it light, Jo. Think of your plans for the future and the store. You have your plans and he has his.

She'd hang on to her contentment and not risk ruining their friendship.

"You look lovely." He kissed her proffered cheek. "And smell good too."

"You're not too shabby yourself." She smoothed his tie. Huddled with him under the umbrella, she caught the scent of Aramis, her favorite cologne, the one she'd given him a few Christmases ago, as they walked into the church.

Inside the packed sanctuary, small groups of women gathered, bouquets of spring color. Children hung on their mothers or ran about as children do, and men in Sunday best greeted each other. The peace of Easter settled over Joann as she and her little group threaded their way to the Kincaid family's usual pew. It was a tight fit. Somehow, Joann ended up wedged between Charles and Mr. Poole. Nathan sat on the very end, next to his dad, and shot Joann a sideways look of amusement. Fine for him. He wasn't smothered by Old Spice and a competing, unnamed cologne. Joann focused her attention on the children's choir. A little girl in front twisted from side to side and the skirt of her ruffled blue dress flared out. She dimpled prettily, basking in the attention. She reminded Joann of Barb, and Joann had to smile.

She wished for an ounce of such self-assuredness. Even as a child, Joann hadn't cared for a spotlight, and certainly didn't have the kind of confidence the tyke onstage displayed. She preferred to work behind the scenes.

After a comforting message about the hope of Easter, the pastor spoke for quite some time about the antiwar demonstration in DC the day before and the civil rights march from Selma to Montgomery, but in a rather vague way, Joann thought. He reminded the congregation to pray for the troops.

Joann closed her eyes and prayed for peace, at home and abroad, and among the members of the small congregation.

Once released, the congregants flowed out of the church doors, Mr. Poole in the lead. Sundays were Dad's favorite, and he usually hung back to visit, but not today. He hustled out with the rest, no doubt to catch Mr. Poole and play a foil to the other man's reticence by instigating conversations with unsuspecting laggers.

Nathan tucked Joann's hand into the crook of his elbow. "May I walk you out?"

"How gentlemanly," Joann teased. "I suppose you may."

They descended the four front steps of the small brick building. A few cautious sunbeams tiptoed across the grass, and the weeds sparkled when the light hit them. If the weather held, the children would get their egg hunt in the park later.

Some distance away, her dad and Mr. Poole strolled along the perimeter of the lawn, the two of them almost indistinguishable from each other in their brown suits.

Barb and Charles made an adorable couple, and a few of the old hens had penned them in, wanting to meet the handsome young man.

Although Charles was handsome enough, Nathan also cut a fine figure in his dark suit. Why did navy look so sophisticated on him but make her appear like a ghost in mourning? She regretted buying all navy for her Easter outfit, then scolded herself for such silly vanity.

Charles and Barb broke away from the ladies and approached Joann.

Charles said, "If your father permits, would it be all right if I took Barb for a turn around the block? We won't be long. Or would that hinder your dinner plans?"

Barb pleaded with her eyes.

Joann pasted on a pleasant expression. Never mind the schedule. "It's fine with me. Meet us at the house." Her gaze flickered to Barb. "Dinner will wait."

Barb nodded her understanding not to linger.

Instead of heading to the gravel parking lot, the couple veered off and took a quiet path.

Nathan and Joann kept their arms linked as they headed to the cars.

He said, "What did you think of the sermon?"

"To be honest, the end confused me a bit when he started talking about the antiwar protest. Was he saying student protests were good or bad?"

Nathan steered her around a puddle. "I think his point was that when a group has a common goal, they can get attention."

"Maybe so. One thing is for certain, people have the right to be heard without fear."

"I agree."

Once they reached the cars, Nathan said, "I need to run home and get something. Don't start dinner without me."

"Not likely." Joann disengaged herself from his arm. She waved at Dad to come over. "We'll wait until everyone gets there, and who knows when Barb and Charles will show up."

***

Stepping into the house felt like entering comfort. The sugary, baked ham smell permeated every corner. Joann promptly started the vegetables warming on the stovetop. Rolls, round and golden, fresh baked the day before, waited on the countertop, and the coconut cake looked divine, if she did say so herself. And she had made the traditional red gelatin mold with sliced strawberries. Dad would expect it, no matter what her little sister said. Besides, Joann liked strawberry mold.

Sweat dampened her brow. Stifling heat filled the kitchen, a combination of the April day and warmth from the oven. Joann wrestled open the window over the sink and propped open the kitchen door, hoping to coax a breeze through.

She heard a car drive up. Two doors slammed. Finally, Barb had shown up to help her out.

Good. Joann would have time to refresh her melting makeup.

"Knock, knock." Nathan peered through the screen door.

Joann's hand flew to her hair, her fingers entangling in the netting and bows. She'd forgotten she still wore her hat. "I thought you were Barb."

"Nope. Just me. And Dad."

Mr. Poole poked his head around Nathan and offered a two-fingered salute.

"And this." Nathan held up a foil-covered dish.

"You didn't have to bring anything!" Her gestures too large, she waved them inside, no doubt a perfect imitation of an unexpectedly rousted hen, ruffled, flustered, and startled by the intrusion into her kitchen. "Come in, come in."

Dirty pots and pans littered the counter, and Joann flushed. She hadn't expected company to traipse through the kitchen, though Nathan and his dad probably didn't think of themselves as such. But the place was such a mess.

Why hadn't she told Nathan to come through the front?

Before church, Barb had set the table with the Shelly china. The blue flowers decorating the old-fashioned set were decidedly spring-like, perfect for Easter.

At least that was done.

Palms flat against her apron front, she said, "Dad's over at the store, getting extra prizes for the kids' egg hunt. Someone is stopping by to pick them up."

Mr. Poole leaned back and his unbuttoned jacket gaped open. He hooked his thumbs in tan suspenders. "I'll mosey on over there, I suppose." He glanced from Nathan to Joann, neither of whom spoke a word. With a quick nod and a noisy clearing of his throat, he turned on his heel and headed out the kitchen door.

The clock on the wall drew Joann's eyes like a magnet. It was gone one thirty already.

She said, "Surely Barb and Charles will be here soon."

"What can I do to help?" Relaxed and comfortable, Nathan leaned against the counter, not at all perturbed by Joann's time watching.

His presence soothed her and she left off fiddling with the pots. The dinner would be fine. Anytime Nathan appeared, her load lightened, and she realized she needn't over concern herself about the mess. It wasn't important.

She gave him a smile. "Everything's ready. You could help me carry the food to the table."

"Happy to." Still holding his dish, he headed for the dining room.

"Wait a minute," she called out. "What do you have there?

Proudly, he peeled back the foil and revealed a congealed mold, as red as hers, with strawberries. Unlike hers, his had layers of creamy white filling, bananas, and whole pecans arranged on top. Arranged, not dumped. A far cry from the strawberry gelatin mold she'd prepared. Hers was plain and a few chunks had come out when she'd unmolded it onto a platter. She'd meant to send Barb across the street for Dream Whip to cover the less than perfect parts.

Nathan's face fell. "What's wrong? Don't you still like strawberries?"

"I do! I love them." She pecked his cheek. "Thank you. It looks delicious." Breaking into a grin wide enough to rival the Cheshire cat, she rubbed exaggerated circles on her stomach. "Can't wait to taste it. I wonder where Barb and Charles could be?"

As soon as Nathan left the kitchen, Joann moved her lumpy strawberry mold from the top shelf of the Frigidaire to the bottom of the back shelf and hid it behind a brown paper bag of oranges.

CHAPTER FIVE

Joann ducked into the bathroom and disentangled the bows from her hair, repairing the damage to her hairdo as best she could.

By the time she emerged, Nathan had bussed most of the food to the table, including the ham. Joann arranged serving spoons and placed a carving knife by the dishes.

Hovering over the food, Nathan inhaled deeply.

Joann pursed her lips in mock disapproval and wagged a finger at him. "If you keep it up, you might burst a lung."

Not moving away from the food, Nathan lolled his head to the side and reverted to his teenage self, giving a fake groan. "I'm starving."

"I'm pretty sure you'll live. Come on. Let's go see where everyone is."

Joann headed through the house, and Nathan came alongside her. For the barest moment, his hand brushed hers, but she couldn't tell if it was intentional. She loved to hold hands with Nathan at the movies, or on walks. But holding hands in front of their parents? They might get ideas. They might start giving advice. The kind that came with expectations, and dad was such a traditionalist.

The thought of a confrontation and the resulting clash of those expectations between the men in her life made her want to fan herself.

Dabbing at the sweat beading her upper lip, Joann approached the front window and peered out. Mr. Poole and Dad stood chatting under the big pecan tree in the front yard.

Joann bit the side of her thumbnail, but clasped her hands together before Nathan could see. Since grade school days, he'd teased her about biting her thumbs, and she hardly did it anymore.

She faced him. "Barb and Charles are nowhere in sight. Do you suppose they had car trouble?"

"Should I drive over to the church and see?"

Joann opened her mouth to reply, but just then the two older men came through the door.

Dad boomed, "Something smells good."

Grinning his agreement, Mr. Poole rocked side to side a few times. "It sure does."

Before Joann could explain Barb hadn't arrived yet, the couple drove up in Charles's flashy red coupe.

Nathan bent close to her ear. "Your sister has perfect timing."

Joann gave an unladylike snort. "By the skin of her teeth. As usual." She spoke to the three men. "Looks like you men won't have to wait on your dinner much longer."

With hearty approval, Mr. Poole and Dad made hasty tracks to the dining room, the pace faster than the leisurely stroll they'd displayed earlier. Nathan followed them.

The open floor plan of the living room and dining area gave Joann a good view of the front door as she placed napkins on the table. Barb and Charles came in, hand in hand. Barb met Joann's eyes and blushed deep pink, her high color contrasting with Charles's pale-as-paper complexion. He let go of Barb, but instead of maintaining space, he took her elbow and kept her arm firmly in his grasp. The air crackled around them. Even from across the room, the electricity lifted the hairs on her arms.

Something was up between those two.

Joann glanced from the couple to her father, but he didn't seem to notice anything. Wasn't paying attention, in fact. The two older men remained on their feet, talking about fishing. Joann's gaze snagged on Nathan, and his brow wrinkled.

Nathan peeled away from Dad and Mr. Poole and came to stand beside Joann, his eyes following the lovebirds. He pitched his voice low. "They make a nice couple."

"Do you think so?" Joann tracked the pair as they circled the table, staying as close together as two scoops on a double-dip cone.

Her feet itched to go after Barb and drag her to the powder room, ask what had happened between her and Charles on the walk, but dinner waited on the table.

She and Barb would have a good sit down after all the guests left and the egg hunt concluded. By then, it would be time for pajamas and a gab session. It had been a while. An ache pinched at her, brought on by holiday wistfulness, no doubt.

Almost absently, she said to Nathan, "Sit wherever you like."

"I'd like to sit by you, if it's all right."

Ready to change the odd mood Barb had brought in, Joann turned to him, a teasing comment on her lips, but the seriousness in his dark brown eyes stopped her.

Her mouth went dry, but she managed to say, "That would be very nice."

One corner of his mouth quirked up, and she felt foolish for reading anything into his statement. Of course he wanted to sit by her. What of it? Where else would he sit? She'd probably misread him. If she'd misread him, maybe she'd misread Barb.

"Glad we're all here." His friendly tone held an edge a stranger wouldn't detect.

It was almost a relief. She wasn't imagining things. Dad had noticed something, whether the lateness or the couple's coziness with each other. Barb would likely get an earful later.

Dad continued, "Let us say the blessing."

Everyone scrambled to find seats and bowed their heads. Dad said a short prayer, no doubt in deference to the delay in the meal.

As soon as the group murmured "Amen" and Dad had sliced the ham, Joann encouraged Nathan and Mr. Poole to take larger helpings.

"There's plenty more." She scooped a serving of green peas.

It was halfway to her plate when Barb said, "We have something to tell you."

Her teeth flashed in a smile bigger than any she'd worn lately, but a certain tilt of her head and the inflection in her voice caused Joann to freeze.

Charles leaned forward. For a fraction of a second, a tiny vee creased the spot between his brows, then disappeared. Joann blinked, unsure of what she'd seen.

Bouncing in her chair, Barb blurted out, "We're getting married!" She withdrew her hand from her lap and held it out, wiggling her fingers. On her left hand, a diamond winked.

The serving spoon Joann held hit the table. Peas rolled across the tablecloth. Joann's mouth dropped open. She swiveled her head around to her father, but instead of the red-faced explosion she expected, he wore a grin to rival Barb's.

He boomed out, "Congratulations!"

Mr. Poole lifted his tea glass in a toast.

The men all descended on Charles, pounding his back and grasping him by the shoulders.

Joann stared at her sister. When had this happened? She took in the scene. Clearly, the happy couple had had a conversation with Dad. Joann had been both big sister and mother to Barb, but Barb hadn't said a word to her.

Neither had Dad.

It was like falling flat and getting the air knocked out of her lungs. She lifted her hand to her forehead, felt the mush of peas smear her skin.

Green splotches stained the tablecloth. They might never come out. Gathering errant peas one by one, Joann dropped them onto her plate.

"Joann. Jo. Here, let me help." Barb swept some of the tiny vegetables into her hand, but Joann whisked her china plate away. During the hubbub, she'd gotten to her feet without realizing it.

She spun on her heel and headed to the kitchen.

The peas went into the trash, and if it hadn't been the good Shelly china, the blue-flowered plate would've followed.

"Jo," Barb said.

Joann didn't turn around. "Go to the dining room, Barb. We have guests. I'll be out in a moment. Can you please make sure everyone has a napkin?"

"Jo."

"I wish you had told me." Joann gave a strangled laugh. "I guess now I know why you haven't been keen on improving the store. You planned on leaving."

"That's not fair."

It wasn't, Joann admitted to herself, but the news had gobsmacked her. More than that, she hadn't paid attention to the gap, no, the *chasm*, opening in the relationship between her and her sister. How could Barb have kept such a secret from her?

Because Joann hadn't paid attention.

Suddenly wobbly, she held on to the countertop with a death grip. "You're right. I'm surprised, is all." And hurt. "I'll be out in a minute to join everyone. We'll talk later."

"If you're sure." Barb's voice was quiet.

Not turning around, Joann gave a stiff nod. She felt unbalanced, unsteady on her feet as if one side of their home had suddenly shifted, tilting the floor.

She knew when Barb left, the same way she knew when Nathan entered.

He came up behind her and rested a strong hand on her shoulder.

Not now.

He meant to be a support, but she needed to gather her wits and deal with her emotions, not fall into his arms. Better to stand on your own feet rather than lean on someone who might decide not to be there the next day.

"Just need to get a dish towel." She choked out a laugh. "So stupid to drop the peas." She ducked from beneath his grip and opened the nearest drawer. Silverware. Barb's news had so unnerved her she couldn't find her way in her own kitchen.

"Hey." Nathan turned her around. "What's wrong? Don't you like Charles?"

"Like him?" Joann snorted. "I don't know him." Her vision blurry from unshed tears, she gazed at Nathan. "Barb didn't tell me."

"Ah." Nathan nodded as if he understood and Joann suppressed the urge to smack him. As an only child, he had no idea. Plus, he was a man. What did men know about the bond between sisters?

Nathan reached for her, but she twisted away. Looking as helpless as a lost little boy, he shoved his hands into his pockets and hunched his shoulders. "What can I do to help?"

"Nothing."

Joann ground the heels of her hands into her eyes and one of her fake eyelashes fell off. It landed on her chest. Taking one look at Nathan, she burst into tears.

He gathered her in for a hug, and she couldn't resist.

"Of all the stupid things to finally cry over." She snuffled and allowed herself to hide her face in his broad chest for a moment.

Nathan patted her back.

Drawing away, she said, "I guess I'd better go repair my face. Tell them I'll be out soon."

He released her. "Are you sure you're okay?"

"Sure."

If life had taught her one thing, it was to carry on.

Back in the dining room, she smiled and congratulated the couple. And at the end of the meal, she managed to choke down a piece of the coconut cake.

Long after the sun had gone down, Joann sat on her bed alone. The heart to heart with Barb had never happened, and now it was too late.

CHAPTER SIX

In the early quiet of the next morning, a nightgown-clad Joann sat upright in bed, flipping through her Bible, but found nothing that spoke to her hurt. Getting married might be the expected thing. It was natural. But it felt as if Barb had betrayed her. While Barb hadn't exactly snuck around with Charles, neither had she gushed about the relationship. In fact, she'd spoken less of Charles than she had of her school crushes. Three weeks ago, Barb had been full of ideas about the store. But truth be told, those ideas may have come about by Joann's prompting. She'd so wanted them to stay together, to carry on the way they always had, depending on each other and working together.

When had Barb abandoned their plans?

When had her dreams changed?

Running the store without her sister seemed an impossible task, but if Joann didn't step up and keep the store going, everything her family had worked so hard to build would crumble and disappear.

Joann put her Bible on the nightstand. She bowed her head.

Lord,

Help me. This is too big for me.

In the silence of the sleeping house, she waited for more words to come, or a flash of clarity, but neither surfaced. When the first birds began the morning song, she lifted her head. Slowly, she dressed, waiting perhaps, for her family to wake, but no one did.

May as well go to the store.

The old building greeted her, the intermingling scents of breads, fresh foods, along with a hint of pipe tobacco, stirring her heart. It was more home than home was and always had been, even before mother had left. Since they were small, Joann and Barb had played jacks in the storeroom and figured solutions to math homework while they sat at the front counter. Joann had imagined Barb would marry a local boy, someone who understood what being a Kincaid meant, perhaps join the business and help keep the family tradition going.

That wouldn't happen now.

She snapped on the radio and let the low strains of a gospel music hour soothe her.

The jangle of Dad's keys as they turned in the lock on the store's front door announced his arrival. With one foot over the threshold, he stopped short. "Hey, there. I thought you were still in bed."

"Nope." Joann plugged in the percolator and set out the cups. The regulars would expect hot coffee, fresh newspapers, and the latest gossip. She set the powdered creamer and an empty blue tin can by the mugs. The coffee was free, but folks would drop in a nickel if they felt inclined to.

"Well, I could've done that." Dad shifted on his feet and scratched behind his ear.

Joann dusted off her hands. "Now you won't have to."

"All right."

Joann found shelves to organize and floors to sweep until the morning bunch started dribbling in. Early birds gave way to morning shoppers. The hands on the wall clock behind the register ticked past eight before Barb showed, Joann noted sourly.

Barb dropped a coin into the piggy bank planter Joann had placed by the register along with a handwritten notice bearing the words: Donations for Morrison Health Clinic for the Blind.

Barb said, "Looks like it's almost full. People are so generous."

Joann swept a pile of dust into a pan and dumped it, whacking the side of the small trashcan harder than necessary. "That's how it is in a small town. People stick together around here."

"Look, I get it," Barb hissed. "You're mad. What I don't get is why."

The group of men playing dominoes and shooting the breeze near the coffee station all stopped talking. Apparently, a private conversation between sisters beat dominoes for entertainment.

"Girls." Dad frowned.

Joann kicked herself for not moving the checker table outside. April was plenty warm enough. On second thought, no doubt Dad would've got on her case about it.

Dredging up her sweetest smile, she said, "I need to pull some stock." She tugged at the hem of her apron and squared her shoulders.

Joann strode to the back of the store, down the hall, past the one bathroom, the office, and the breakroom, all the while trying to keep her temper. At the back were two storerooms, one for the perishable items and the other for the rest of the stock.

She fished her keys out and wrestled open the door to the storeroom for nonperishables, went in, and closed the door quickly. If only she could shut out all her troubles. Inhaling the stale air, she pinched the bridge of her nose and leaned her back against the wall. She hadn't meant to set Barb off.

Joann was nothing but a ball of prickles today.

Right inside the entrance, a clipboard hung on a nail and she snatched it down, flipping through the invoice pages. Joann stared at the writing, then the shelves of foodstuffs. She sniffed and wiped at her eyes, muttering, "Silly dust making my eyes water." She ignored the fact that she'd been working in the room the day before with no trouble at all.

It was too hard to figure out what stock they might need on the floor. Instead, she began an inventory, a job she could drag out for as long as needed. Starting on one end of an aisle, she listlessly began counting packages of rice.

Barb's muffled voice came through the wood paneled door. "Jo. Can I come in?"

Joann didn't stop with her pretend inventory, but raised her voice and said, "Yup."

The door opened.

Joann retrieved a tissue from her pocket and wiped her nose. "Dusty back here."

Barb came in, closing the door with a soft bump. "Jo. Don't be upset."

"Why would I be upset?"

"I know you don't like Charles."

"Don't like Charles? Why does everyone think I don't like the man?" She balled up the tissue and pushed it deep into her apron pocket.

"Then why are you acting this way?"

Joann picked up a box of rice and shook it, then turned it around, squinting at the label.

"Stop avoiding."

"Avoiding?" Joann plopped the box down. "I'm avoiding? What about my sister avoiding so much as a hint she was serious about some Air Force guy?"

Do not cry.

Joann furiously blinked back tears. Her voice wobbled. "You used to tell me everything."

Hugging herself, Barb slumped against the wall. "I know." Her lips turned down. "But I thought you wouldn't approve. Every time I tried to talk about Charles, you acted like you didn't want to hear. Jealous, almost."

Joann snorted. "Jealous? Don't be ridiculous." She shuffled random boxes of beans around on the shelf.

"Why can't you just be happy for me?"

Because you left me out and blew all our future plans for the store out of the water without talking to me.

But maybe those had never been Barb's plans. Not really.

"I don't know." Joann picked at a misplaced label stuck to the shelf. "Maybe I am jealous. Jealous of Charles." She turned around. "What am I supposed to do without you? What about the store? We always talked about when we would be the bosses."

From the other side of the wall, the muted scolding of a mother filtered into the storeroom, followed by a child's cry.

A pensive Barb focused on the small window over Joann's shoulder, but Joann couldn't fathom the meaning behind her sister's demeanor.

Joann prodded, "You and me. Isn't that right?"

In a tone so quiet Joann had to strain to hear, Barb said, "Things change." The faraway look evaporated, and she lifted her chin.

Something in the line of Barb's jaw reminded Joann of the delicate china platter she'd washed and put away the night before. A feather's touch of fear tickled the back of her neck.

Joann crossed the room and peered into Barb's face. "What things?"

Clasping her hands at her waist, Barb dipped her head. "I love him, Jo. That's what changed. I can't help it."

Her sister, the hopeless romantic. But real life wasn't an Elvis love song.

"Are you sure?"

"I think so."

"Oh, Barb. You need to be sure."

"But don't you always say nothing is certain?"

This was true. Joann had the tendency toward practicality and examining things in the clear light of day.

"Some things are certain." The words came slowly, thoughtfully, as Joann picked her way through the conversation. "Family, for one. I'll always have your back, no matter what." She smiled. "Even when I'm mad at you." She leaned forward and grasped Barb by the arms, touching foreheads with her sister. "Faith, for another."

Joann kicked herself for never talking to Barb about Charles's religion. Barb would never marry an unbeliever, would she?

She drew back and let go of Barb, but stayed close, all the fire gone out of her. "What does Charles think about God and church?"

"Don't worry. He promised me we would raise our family in the church." She got all misty-eyed. "He told me he prayed and begged God to send him a girl like me."

The viselike tightness in Joann's scalp receded to a tingle. It was a comfort to know Charles had a strong faith, but concern still clung on like a burr. "I only hope he'll follow through."

She wouldn't tread into the question of denominations. Surely Dad wouldn't have given his blessing if there had been an issue.

Barb crossed her arms and blew out a puff of air. "Can't you just be happy for me?"

"Of course I can." Joann frowned. "Or at least I promise to try. But don't shut me out." She twisted a strand of Barb's honey-gold hair around her finger, the way she used to do when they were small and couldn't bear to sleep apart. "But I'll miss you when you get married." She let go of Barb's hair and put an arm around her shoulder, giving her a shake. "But the wedding won't be for ages, yet, right?"

Barb pressed her lips together. Slowly, she said, "We don't want to wait too long. Who knows what might happen next week, or even tomorrow?"

"Sounds like you want to get married this afternoon!"

Barb said nothing.

"I suppose you'll have to talk to Pastor." Before their pastor agreed to marry a couple, he always had a talk with the pair, and required them to attend classes for several weeks. Previously, Joann had thought it overbearing, but it sounded like wisdom now.

Barb lifted one shoulder. "We might not get married in our church."

"What? Why on earth not?"

Barb fiddled with her necklace, then tugged her earlobe, a sure tell she was nervous, or about to spill a string of half-truths. "We thought Charles's mother might get upset, feel left out if we got married in the little church down here. She can't travel."

"So you're going to Wisconsin?"

"No, no. Don't worry. I wouldn't get married without you there. I need you to be my bridesmaid."

"Well, then where?"

Barb bit her lip. "The courthouse."

All the air whooshed out of Joann's body. No wedding? No guests? A civil service?

She shook her head. "Dad won't allow it. No way. You won't get his permission for a courthouse wedding."

Instead of backing down, Barb ran a trembling hand along the collar of her shirt and down the bib of her shop apron.

She said, "He's already given it."

"What? That doesn't sound like Dad. He'd love a big wedding, a chance to show you off to the town. What's the rush?"

"Like I said, you never know what tomorrow may bring." Barb's fingers crept to her earlobe again.

Seconds ticked by. Nothing stirred in the room except the dust motes flying around, propelled by the sisters' breathing.

Barb looked at Joann from under her lashes and away again. Guilt? What would she have to feel guilty about? Joann's mind flashed to Barb's recent emotional upsets and bouts of sickness and lethargy. The clues slotted into place. Joann gasped. How had she not seen it before?

"Oh, Barb. Tell me you're not pregnant."

Barb's face crumpled.

Joann wrapped her arms around her baby sister, shushing her, but no amount of sisterly comfort could change the future set in motion.

CHAPTER SEVEN

Who did a girl call to talk over things when her closest female confidant was the very person she needed to talk about? For four days, she avoided mentioning the upcoming marriage or the pregnancy to Barb. Instead, she alternated between fussing over her, bringing her cold drinks and petting her, and fighting the urge to deliver a screaming lecture.

During Joann's lunch break on Friday, she stared at the phone in the office.

Never before had she not known what to say or do when Barb ran into trouble. She had to talk to someone.

Phoning a man for personal reasons wasn't done, but Nathan was an exception. The day before, he'd made the vegetable delivery as usual but Joann hadn't been ready to talk then. She tried not to overthink the fact that she'd never called him for anything so serious and sensitive before.

He answered right away.

"I need to talk to you. It's not an emergency or anything." She twisted the curly telephone cord in her finger.

"Should I come over later? We could sit on the porch swing and talk."

The walls may as well sprout ears for all the privacy the porch swing offered. "No. Let's go to the pictures at the drive-in. Grab a bite." She sounded forward. Prickles of embarrassment spread over her chest.

Nathan didn't seem to mind, though. In fact, she could hear the smile in his voice.

He said, "Sounds good. Better than good. I've been so busy with surveying a section of the property and drawing up plans, I've neglected you."

Instead of contradicting his observation as she usually would, Joann let the comment slide past.

Softer, Nathan continued, "Seems like both of us have been busy even when we're in the same room. I've missed spending time with you."

She blushed even harder at his confession. She'd missed him too, but wasn't about to say so and get sidetracked. As if she could.

She said, "All right. Pick me up at seven thirty?"

"Sure thing."

They said their goodbyes and Joann set the receiver gently in the cradle.

Nathan really was a great friend.

The end of the day neared, and Joann rushed to finish her work, telling Dad and Barb she had a date. As expected, Barb volunteered to take care of any stragglers and do the final closing.

Joann went home and changed into a clean blouse, refreshed her makeup, then snatched her new, narrow silk scarf from her vanity, tying it on as a final touch. The theme song for *The Big Valley* made its way upstairs, blaring from the set in the living room. Dad was home. If someone didn't fix him a dinner in a hurry, he'd eat nothing but crackers and jam. She hustled down to the kitchen and popped a frozen dinner into the oven. Those dinners came in handy, and Dad liked them. Or at least he never complained.

As soon as it was heated through, she walked the meal of meatloaf, potatoes, and green peas to her dad and put it on the metal TV tray next to his recliner. Caught up in the show, he barely noticed. With his swollen, sock-clad feet on the footrest and his balding head tilted back, he looked the picture of the working man after a hard day's labor.

"I'll be back by eleven. Eleven thirty at the latest."

Attention not wavering from the set, Dad said, "All right. Have a nice date."

All of a sudden, he swiveled his gaze to her. She felt like a bug pinned to a board.

He said, "You know, I approve of Nathan. He's a respectful young man."

Had he emphasized *respectful* the tiniest bit? Or was she reading too much into an offhand comment? She didn't know how much her dad had guessed about Barb's situation. The comment could've been a negative reference to Charles. Or something else entirely. Or nothing at all.

Had Dad somehow overheard her conversation with Nathan? She hadn't thought so at the time.

The last thing Joann needed to worry about right now was her relationship with Nathan. The family had enough going on without opening another can of worms.

Flustered, she went to the kitchen and prepared Dad's glass of sweet tea, but before she took it to him, she poured herself a glass and gulped it down.

Back in the living room, she told him, "I think I'll sit out front for a minute to cool off."

He grunted in reply.

In the foyer, she stopped to adjust her skirt. When she looked up, she caught sight of the plaque on the wall with a passage from Proverbs inscribed on it. The plaque Dad had put up the day after mother left.

Trust in the LORD with all thine heart; and lean not unto thine own understanding. In all thy ways acknowledge him, and he shall direct thy path. Proverbs 3: 5-6

It was good advice, and she knew she needed God's wisdom.

Her mother had not followed God's ways, to be sure. Or at least Dad had said so. There may have been good reason for her to leave, but she had never come back or told Joann and Barb where she'd gone. A cousin had told Dad she'd moved to Philadelphia and was fine, happy living there with her new husband.

If Joann knew anything about God's ways, caring for your family and honoring your responsibilities was high on the list. Joann did her level best to live by those values. No one could say otherwise.

Still, every time she passed the plaque she felt a niggle of guilt, though she didn't understand why. She'd pondered it before and hadn't figured it out, so a revelation wasn't likely to come today.

She checked her watch. By her Timex, she had a good fifteen minutes before Nathan would pick her up. Slipping off her heels, she sat in the old wooden rocker and set it in motion with a gentle nudge of her foot as she considered how much to tell Nathan about Barb.

Please God, show me what to do.

Two boys of about eight years old ran alongside the road, taking advantage of the evening sunshine and chasing each other in the overgrown spring grass. Their feet crushed the leaves, releasing the tang of tender new growth.

She waited until the children passed, but no clarity came. Her thoughts remained as tangled as the weeds. An answer to her prayer hadn't come.

Nathan drove up in his truck, and Joann waved at him. She ran barefoot to meet him. "Stay here. I'll go get my purse." She wriggled her toes. "And my shoes."

She was back in a flash and hopped in. The bench seat squeaked, and a spring jabbed at her rear until she shifted on the blanket covering the upholstery.

Nathan dressed for the occasion in a trim-fitting brown dress jacket over a green mock turtleneck. The outfit brought out the warmth in his brown eyes and seemed to make the copper highlights in his hair brighter.

It was enough to make a girl want to weave her fingers in those wavy locks and forget what she wanted to talk about.

At the drive-in, they ordered food and settled in. Nathan had eaten half his hotdog before Joann broached the subject of Charles.

Studiously avoiding direct eye contact, she concentrated on her burger, picking a seed from the bun. "Nathan, do you think you could hang out with Charles one evening and get a feel for what he's about?"

The tinny strains of Julie Andrews came through the speaker hooked to Nathan's window, perfectly in sync with the twirling nun on the big screen.

Sweat pricked Joann's palms.

Nathan squinted at her as if she'd asked him to don a tutu and dance along with the movie. "I don't understand what you mean."

A bite of burger stuck in her throat and she took a sip of Tab to help it go down. "See what he's up to, what he thinks about things, you know." Joann laughed and attempted a flippant toss of her hair. "Maybe make a list of his vices."

Nathan recoiled. "You want me to spy on him?"

"No. Not spy. Just find out stuff."

"I see. Don't spy, but spy." The springs in the truck seat creaked as he sat back. "Barb is a grown woman. You can't stop her from getting married if she wants to."

"I know." Joann twiddled with a french fry. Barb wouldn't thank her for telling private matters, but Joann needed Nathan's help. "I'm worried about her."

"What else is new?"

"You don't understand, Nathan. I'm really concerned."

His face darkened, frown lines bracketing his mouth. "Did Charles hurt her?"

"No. No. That's not it."

"Then what?"

She'd intended to confide in him, but couldn't force the words past her frozen lips, couldn't lay bare the details about Barb being in the family way.

Once, an overeager high school suitor had hung about the store, harassing Barb. Dad had told the boy to clear off. He hadn't taken it well. Instead of leaving her alone, the boy had trailed after Barb at school, calling her names and throwing wet pebbles of chewed up gum into her hair. When Nathan had found out about it, he'd punched the guy square in the nose.

They weren't school children anymore, but Nathan still had a protective streak.

And if he found out about the baby, he'd be disappointed. Might even blame Joann for not watching over her sister better.

"Barb has some things going on and I don't know Charles well enough to advise her."

Nathan blew out a breath.

Joann's package of fries slid from her lap as she grabbed his sleeve. "Please, Nathan. I wouldn't ask if it weren't important." She released her grip, leaving a greasy spot on his shirt. "Oh no, look what I've done." Snatching up a napkin, she dabbed at the spot. "Bring your shirt to me tomorrow and I'll scrub it up."

He caught her hands in his. "What's got you so flustered?"

"Please don't ask for details. Just make sure Charles is a good guy." Her chin trembled, and she swallowed hard. "Please."

Nathan's gaze roamed over her features. With a sigh, he brought her hands to his lips and brushed a kiss across her knuckles. "All right."

They watched the movie in silence for a few minutes. A smudge across the windshield blurred her view of the picture, but Joann kept her eyes straight ahead.

Without looking at her, Nathan said, "Is that all you wanted to talk about?"

He sounded hurt.

"I guess."

"Thought maybe you might want to talk about us."

"Us?"

"With Barb getting married, I wondered if it got you to thinking. She *is* younger than you."

A strangled laugh escaped Joann. "Don't worry. Just because my sister wants to get married, don't think I'm in a hurry and plan to drag you down the aisle. We're fine the way we are. I have the store. You have the orchards and the farm to think about." She shook her head. "Other girls might swoon at the idea of white lace and roses, but I promise I won't try to push you into anything."

A fairy-tale wedding had always been a far-off dream, but she was determined to be content with what she had. Even if Nathan decided to get all romantic, how long would his intent last? She'd rather have the comfortable relationship she and Nathan had than deal with the inevitable heartache to come if she got too serious with him.

She wrinkled her nose. "Can you imagine me in a white gown?"

"I can."

What?

Joann's heart thundered. She couldn't have heard him right.

Nathan said, "Why do you think I'm still hanging around this town?"

"The farm. Your orchard. Your Dad."

"I love more than the farm and my dad."

A thousand fluttering sparrows set loose in her chest. What did he expect from her? She couldn't imagine being a farm wife like his mother. Mr. Poole had come home from the war in '45 a changed man and had never been right again, or so they said. Mrs. Poole, a patient, stoic woman with a green thumb, kept the farm going until she got sick.

Joann couldn't keep potted ivy alive.

Now that Nathan had brought up marriage, she fought the urge to open the door and run.

She tried for a carefree tone. "Let's not let things get heavy. We have plenty of time. We're young."

"Not that young." He sounded forlorn.

She wanted to trust him, but marriage? A voice in her head told her to wait and see how long he played this tune. The impulse would pass.

She didn't want to ruin their friendship.

Maybe he was just looking for reassurance, needed to know they were okay. She picked her words carefully.

"I have family obligations right now. And things are so up in the air." She stroked the curls at the base of his neck. "I'm not ready for marriage. Not by a long shot."

Which was true. She'd already settled on what her life was meant to be for the near future, and since Barb had decided to get married, it was up to Joann alone to carry on the family traditions. She couldn't betray her heritage.

He gave her a penetrating look. "Not ready? Is that all there is to it?"

She removed her fingers from his hair. Did he mean what she thought he meant? "There's no one else, if that's what you're insinuating." Like she had time to date other boys.

He scrubbed at his face and pulled at his lower lip, something he hadn't done in years. Not since grief had haunted him the year his mother died.

He said, "Are you sure?"

She bumped him with her knee. "Of course I'm sure."

"As long as you don't throw me over, I'm fine with waiting."

Before Joann processed his words, he cradled her head in his palm and his lips met hers. The idea of having Nathan as hers forever, sharing a house in the country with him bloomed in her imagination. She did love him, but truth be told, the idea of belonging to another life, contorting herself into a mold not her own, terrified her. What if it didn't work out?

She should've pulled away, explained she didn't want to make promises, but his touch melted her and rattled her brain.

It was too late. He'd trapped her.

Or maybe she'd trapped herself.

CHAPTER EIGHT

Joann couldn't figure out how—or even if—she should continue the talk with Nathan about their relationship. Conflicting emotions plagued her. One thing for certain, she couldn't imagine a life without him. She just didn't know where, exactly, he fit in. Her brain and her heart pulled her in opposite directions.

She sighed as she retrieved a ledger from behind the counter.

Why did it have to be so complicated?

At least she had the distraction of Barb's upcoming wedding. The news had put a smile on many a face, Joann had to admit. And Barb seemed happy. Joann prayed she stayed so.

Joann scanned the store. Not too many customers at the moment. "Mrs. Delarue?" she called.

Mrs. Delarue popped from behind a shelf of kitchen essentials and guiltily brushed at her apron. It was payday, and she'd been eyeing the pretty new dishtowels all week. If the woman didn't buy one for herself, Joann would tuck one away for her, a thank-you gift for all her help with the wedding reception. The minute Mrs. Delarue had heard about the preparations, she'd offered to lend a hand.

Joann said, "Follow me back while it's quiet and I'll get you squared away."

Once they got to the back office, Mrs. Delarue interlaced her fingers and brought them to her chest. She burbled, "I'm so happy for Barb, and I can't wait to get busy with the decorations."

For the reception, they'd cleared space upstairs in the store. No time to arrange another location and it seemed more workable than squeezing everyone into the house. The store was practically home anyway.

"Are you sure you don't mind?" Joann handed Mrs. Delarue her pay envelope.

"Mind? Don't be silly, dear! I wouldn't have volunteered if I didn't want to do it. Why, I love decorating. And weddings." The woman's button eyes turned into happy crescents above the apples of her cheeks. "May is such a wonderful month for a wedding."

Joann couldn't help but smile in return.

Mrs. Delarue said, "A little celebration never hurt anyone." She separated out a few bills for pin money and slipped them into her bra before putting the pay envelope into her pocket.

"I don't know how I ever managed without you." Joann meant every word.

With a crinkled forehead and a half smile, Mrs. Delarue waved the comment aside, but Joann could tell she was pleased.

Later, Joann thought about pin money, and how she never wanted to hide cash or skim from the grocery budget just to have something to call her own. Nathan would certainly be a generous and fair man. Joann grimaced. The idea of another person pulling her purse strings for the rest of her life didn't sit well.

But that's the way things worked when you were married. Another reason to be content with remaining single, she reminded herself.

***

The day before Barb was to be married, she burst into the kitchen wearing a wedding dress. "Jo! Look at this."

The frosting knife Joann held clattered to the floor. White cream frosting left a swath of sweet goo on the linoleum. "Barb! What did you make me do?"

Tears streaking her face, Barb wrung her hands.

Joann's heart jumped into her throat. "What's wrong?"

"I tore Mary June's dress!" Barb wailed.

Was that all? Joann laid a hand on her chest and deflated with relief. The fear of Charles bailing had popped into her mind. She banished the thought.

She scanned the simple cream dress from hem to empire waist to sweetheart neckline, but saw nothing amiss. "Where?"

Barely lifting her arms, Barb squeezed her eyes closed and pointed to the underarm area on the right. Skin showed through the gaping underarm seam.

"But you and Mary June are the exact same size." The words were hardly out of Joann's mouth before she realized why her sister's chest had suddenly expanded. The girls hadn't spoken of the baby since the day in the storage room, not for lack of Joann trying.

Frozen as a statue, Barb remained in the middle of the kitchen, her face all scrunched up. "What am I going to do?"

"Never mind," Joann cooed, wiping the mascara from Barb's face with a paper towel. "I can fix it. Look, if you don't stop crying, you'll have red, swollen, frog eyes. You don't want to have frog eyes in your pictures tomorrow, do you?" Joann pressed the soggy paper towel into Barb's hand.

Barb hiccupped and blew her nose, unable to hide a tiny smile. "No. You're right. Sorry."

Joann maneuvered Barb and checked all the seams. The edges of the fabric would fit back together, barely. "It's not so bad. We can fix it. No one will know the difference."

"Are you sure it won't show?"

"It should be fine as long as you don't lift your arms."

"Gosh. I hope I remember. Why did I even worry about a wedding dress?"

Because you only get married once.

At least that's the way it was supposed to be.

Closing her eyes for a second, Joann made a fervent wish for Barb to have a happy, solid marriage lasting the rest of her life.

Then Joann opened her eyes and took charge.

"Go take the dress off." She pointed to the patches of buttercream icing on the floor. "And watch your step. I'll get a needle and thread and meet you upstairs in your room."

Once Barb left, Joann examined the cake. No damage done.

Mrs. Canfield's Cookery Book lay on the table, open. A tiny blob of icing marred the corner of the page and Joann wiped it off with a dry dishcloth. Chiding herself for leaving the book on the table, she closed it and placed it on top of the Frigidaire.

The frosting-covered floor could wait.

Joann retrieved the wicker sewing box from the bottom shelf of the linen closet and tapped on Barb's door before going in. Barb had wriggled out of the dress. Joann walked over to the bed, pushed aside a pile of clothes and magazines to make room, and sat on the floral bedspread. The pink floral décor had been a gift for Barb's twelfth birthday. A pang of wistfulness struck Joann. This might be the last time she'd do any mending for her little sister.

How corny to get sentimental over such things.

Brusquely, Joann said, "Let me see the dress."

"I can't believe I tore it."

"It'll be fine." Joann carefully spread the fabric, concentrating on her mending. She'd make it right for her sister. "You'll be lovely. Do you have a new pair of panty hose? What about shoes?"

She sewed as Barb rummaged in the clothes closet.

For the first time in a long time, Joann let her thoughts dwell on her mother. Bitterness over her absence had plagued Joann during her teen years, but today she only felt sadness when her mother came to mind.

Mother had missed out.

After finding suitable shoes, Barb sorted through her lingerie drawer. She grabbed several pairs of hose, stretching them longways to check for runners. They could get new from the store, but Joann didn't say so. It seemed they were both attempting to stay busy.

Joann wove the needle in and out of the seam, focusing on the tiny stitches. "Is it only the dress you were crying about? You can change your mind, you know. You don't have to go through with the marriage."

While technically true, in the real here and now, what choice did Barb have? There was the baby to think of.

Barb sat on the bed beside Joann and crumpled the hosiery she held in her lap. "No. I want to get married."

The last stitch in place, Joann knotted the thread and snipped off the tail. Unable to hold her tumbling thoughts in check any longer, she blurted, "Do you love him truly, Barb? Because if you don't, you can call it off. We can figure things out."

"I love him. It's not just because of, you know. I'd want to marry him anyway." Barb turned a shade of dark red to rival her something-borrowed, Grandmother Kincaid's ruby pinky ring. "I don't want you to have the wrong idea about Charles. It's not … well, it wasn't all his fault, you know. I wish we'd waited, but it just happened and we love each other. I don't want anyone else."

Joann began to cry, and not a gentle, pretty cry either. Whether the tears came from disappointment in Barb or relief that the couple was sincerely in love, she didn't know. "Why didn't you tell me about it? I mean, before?" She sniffed and wiped her drippy nose with the back of one hand.

Barb hung her head. "I don't know."

What came out of Joann's mouth next even shocked herself. "They're going to say it's because you have no mother."

"That's not true." Barb clutched Joann's free hand in a fierce grip. "Don't even think such a thing." Barb stuck her nose in the air. "Let them gossip. I don't care because I know I have the best big sister in the world. No mom could be better."

CHAPTER NINE

The birds were barely up when Joann added an extra spoon of Folger's to the percolator and plugged it in. Thumps and bumps from upstairs indicated Barb was up. They wouldn't need to leave for hours yet, but who could sleep? As she waited for the coffee, Joann stole a moment to sit on the porch. The red-painted sky predicted storms. Joann prayed for a clear day, a silly thing to ask for, then changed her prayer to one asking wedding blessings.

She wondered if her mother had had any inkling on her wedding day how things would turn out. There had been plenty of arguments before Mother quietly packed and drove away one day while Dad stood in the driveway glowering, arms folded across his chest. Joann didn't know much about marriage, but for certain it was hard work. Whatever came, Barb would need all the prayers she could get.

By the time Joann finished a cup of coffee, ran an iron over Dad's shirt, and helped Barb find hairpins, Nathan was knocking at the back door.

She needed his help to move the cake over for the reception, and it would be the first time they'd been alone since he'd turned serious. Anxious over more than Barb's wedding, Joann smoothed her hair before opening the door.

She smiled. "Thanks for coming to help."

"Not a problem."

He gave her his typical devilish grin and her shoulders relaxed. There would be no heavy talk today.

Maybe never, a tiny voice whispered inside her head, leaving a soft bruise in the center of her heart. She reminded herself she hadn't any right to be hurt. It was for the best.

He draped his jacket over a chair and nodded at Joann, his eyes lingering on her figure. "You look nice."

"Did you notice my shoes? Going for a new look." She'd slipped on her old saddle shoes for the cake-moving operation. Forcing a grin, she waggled one foot. "For this job, heels wouldn't do."

She'd change footwear later. Getting the cake upstairs came before vanity.

"You look good in anything."

Typical male response. But nice.

Joann rolled a cart to the counter. "Ready to help me transfer?"

They lifted the two-tiered cake and set it on the cart. Perhaps the cake was excessive, but Joann felt Barb deserved the nicest reception possible.

She said, "I'll push. You hold it steady."

A bright, cloudless day had emerged. No thunderstorms, thank goodness. All disasters, large or small, stayed away, for which Joann was grateful.

They got the cart inside the store without a hitch, but getting the cake upstairs would take strategy.

Since Nathan was taller, she went backward toward the stairs, keeping the cake stable as she put a foot behind her to feel the next step up. "This is easier than I'd imagined."

"We work well together."

"We do." She kept her attention on the cake and her feet, instead of the guy in front of her. He cut a fine figure, even with his sleeves rolled up and concentration wrinkling his forehead.

When they reached the top and finally set the cake on the table safe and sound, she breathed a sigh of relief.

The cake transfer out of the way, other concerns crowded her mind. She turned to Nathan. "I'm still worried about Barb. Did you find out anything about Charles?"

Nathan rapped his knuckles on the table, a nervous gesture. "I met Charles for coffee last night. He seemed a pretty stand-up guy, if a bit stiff." Nathan frowned. "I wasn't sure what you wanted to know, but he loves his mother, has always gone to church, and enlisted right out of high school." He paused. "I hope that's enough for you." He ran a finger along the table, avoiding her gaze, but one raised eyebrow gave away a hint of judgment.

It reminded her of the time she'd sneaked ice cream and sodas from the store for them.

Such a rule follower.

Ignoring the implied criticism in his words, she said, "Thank you." She scrubbed her forehead. "It's hard not to worry." And it was hard to keep herself from spilling the beans about the baby, but she shut her mouth tight.

Nathan narrowed his eyes, trying to read her. His expression cleared as if he'd cracked the last clue of a crossword puzzle. "This is more than you not wanting to let her go."

"Don't be silly." Joann started toward the stairs. "Come on. We don't want to be late. I have to finish getting ready."

"Hey." He caught her arm and gently swung her around. "You know I'll always look out for Barb. She's like a little sister to me." His earnest brown eyes met hers.

She leaned into him, and his arm encircled her. They stayed on the top of the landing for a few minutes, surrounded by all the normal smells of the store and the sweet, over-sugared scent of cake, her head resting on his strong shoulder.

His fingertips grazed the side of her face. "We better go."

Joann nodded and took his hand, leading the way.

***

Charles, Barb, Joann, and her dad squeezed into the clerk's office while Nathan waited on a bench in the corridor with Joann's brownie camera in his lap.

The office surroundings felt wrong, but Joann focused on her sister's smile as the clerk asked a couple of questions and then indicated where Joann and her dad could sign as witnesses. Numbly, she took up the pen and shakily scrawled her name, marveling her signature looked as neat as it always did.

Quick as that, the couple were married, the pronouncement and first kiss out of the way. The couple radiated bliss.

Maybe they would be all right.

As soon as they all got outside, Joann stopped on the wide courthouse steps. "We have to get a picture before we leave."

A beaming Charles led Barb off to the side. Joann held out her hand for her camera.

"Oh no." Nathan clutched it to his chest. "You get over there." He lifted his chin, indicating Barb and the others.

"Yes!" A smiling Charles waved her over. "You have to be in the picture."

Joann had never seen him so animated and relaxed, and Barb glowed.

Dad had his arm around Charles. Joann took her place beside her sister and pasted on a smile, squinting in Nathan's direction. The camera clicked.

"One more," Nathan said, snapping the shot right as a gust of wind caught Barb's short veil.

Joann broke off from the group and approached Nathan. "We'd better get back and prepare for the reception."

When they pulled into the lot at the side of the store, two cars were already there.

"Yoo-hoo! Joann!" Cora Lee leaned out of her sedan's window and waved a hanky. "Joann, do you need some help setting up?"

Turning the woman down would provoke a longer conversation. Better to accept the offer. Besides, Mrs. Delarue could surely use extra help.

Joann smiled. "Thank you. Can you wait at the side door? I'll meet you there as soon as I can come through."

Pleasure suffused Cora Lee's face. "Of course."

She sat back, smug. The expression made Joann's hackles rise, but only for a second. If Cora Lee expected to find a morsel of unhappiness between the two newlyweds today, she'd be disappointed.

During the cake cutting, Barb clamped her forearms to her sides, no doubt in fear of ripping the hastily sewn repairs.

Charles fed Barb a bite of cake. A dab of frosting landed on her shoulder and she fussed at him about it, much to the amusement of the gathering.

As soon as people lined up to get cake, Barb whispered in Joann's ear. "Come with me to the house and help me take off this dress before I rip it again."

The girls slipped out, stopping in the kitchen where Joann sponged the frosting off.

Barb nibbled at her pinkie fingernail. "Are you sure we got it all?"

"It's only buttercream. Most brushed right off, and I got the rest."

"I'm a bundle of nerves." Barb let out a high-pitched laugh. "Everything seems so odd. Like it's not real."

Oh, it was real, but Barb didn't need to hear Joann tell her it was too late for second thoughts now. She gave Barb a kiss on the cheek.

As soon as they got into Barb's room, she twisted around and demanded, "Unzip me."

The underarm stitches held, and Barb released a long breath. "I wish I'd worn my Easter dress from the start."

Joann arranged the wedding gown on a padded hanger and hung it up. "Don't get dressed yet. I need to get something from my room."

"What are you up to?" Barb flung a robe on over her slip.

Joann headed across the hall, Barb following.

A baby blue jacket and skirt set hung on a hook, and Joann retrieved it. "For your going-away outfit."

"Oh, Jo. You shouldn't have!"

"I'm not sending you off without a new outfit."

Barb blinked back tears. "You're too good to me."

To avoid crushing the suit, Barb embraced Joann with an awkward, one-armed hug.

Barb stroked the fabric. "This blue is so lovely." She dressed slowly, as if her feet were stuck in molasses. Smoothing her hair, she mused, "Maybe I should take a brush to this and respray it."

Leave it to her sister to dawdle! Maybe her nerves were worse than Joann thought.

"Your hair is fine. It's beautiful." Joann adopted a teasing tone. "There won't be any guests left to see you off if we don't get a move on."

"I don't care, as long as you and Dad are there." The green specks showed in Barb's eyes.

Joann held her baby sister's gaze in the mirror until tears blurred her vision. She grabbed a tissue, scowling. "Why'd you have to go and make me cry?" She dabbed at her eyes. "Come on. Let's rescue Charles. No doubt Cora Lee or Mrs. Delarue has cornered him by now. Or Dad."

The girls laughed through tears, wiping each other's faces, and then headed back to the reception.

Once in the store, they emerged upstairs, greeted by a chorus of cheers. Barb peeled away from Joann's side and joined Charles. He dropped a quick kiss on her lips, provoking hoots from the crowd. A red-faced Charles smiled so big it seemed as if he might show every tooth in his gums.

He handed Barb her bouquet and the younger women lined up, ready to catch.

Mrs. Delarue sidled up to Joann. "Go on and join the other girls. No need to be shy."

Shy wasn't the right word.

Joann joined the pack well behind everyone else. Mary June's sister caught the bouquet.

The gaggle of single ladies dispersed, and Joann found herself face to face with Nathan.

"Your Dad wants to talk to you." He took her hand and wove through the thinning crowd to where her dad entertained a few townspeople.

The minute he spied Joann, he interrupted his story and headed her way, arms outstretched, eyes crinkling. His smile struck Joann to her marrow. The moment deserved to be joyous, but she already felt homesick for Barb. Half of the Kincaid sisters had been erased with a few words.

"I have to show you something," Dad said.

The eager twinkle in his eyes reminded her of Christmas morning when he'd finally let them go downstairs to check their stockings for the goodies Santa had left.

She cast a questioning glance at Nathan, and he gestured as if to shoo her along.

Dad led her past the guests and party setup, over to a quieter area of the store and swept out an arm. "There you go!"

A row of five record players and a shelf with albums took up a small section of the retail space.

Dad leaned close as if sharing a confidence. "Barb told me what to buy."

"When did this happen?"

"I told Barb to keep you busy while Nathan helped me set up the area."

No wonder Barb had dragged her feet! Joann cast a glance at her sister. Barb and Charles, arms linked, happily chatted with another couple.

Flinging his arm around Joann's shoulders, Dad pressed a dry kiss to her temple. "Me and you will make a go of it, hey?" He gave her a little shake. "We'll be all right, won't we? And Nathan will help."

"Oh, Dad." For at least the third time in the space of a day, Joann blinked back tears.

CHAPTER TEN

Even though Barb was only a car drive away in Bossier City, she may as well have been clear across the entire country for how much Joann missed her. After six weeks, Joann still called out for her sister at times, forgetting she wasn't around. The days were busy, but didn't zip by, as busy days should. They stretched long.

It was worse during slow periods.

The morning hadn't been too bad, with people coming in and out to keep her attention squarely on serving customers, except when Nathan had come today to unload delivery trucks. He'd been his silly self, teasing smiles from her with jokes and leaving a jelly jar of wildflowers by the register before Dad had given him a look that had kept Nathan on store tasks since.

By afternoon, few customers remained in the shop and Dad left her to it. With the emptying of the building, oppression hung heavy in the air, unavoidable. Mrs. Delarue sat at the checkers table listlessly stacking rumpled newspapers, reading and rereading the headlines, as if by magic the print might change into less troubling news.

Joann bustled over. "Let me."

It wasn't healthy to bury one's head in the sand, but Mrs. Delarue didn't need to rehash the news. A constant, low level of dread plagued Joann. She couldn't imagine what Mrs. Delarue experienced, with Matty in the Army.

In a news conference, a spokesperson had said Westmoreland had been given authority to commit

American ground troops, but the White House denied the new combat mission. The conflicting information made Joann wonder who was in charge.

Sometimes she wished she could ignore the TV and the papers. But if everyone took such an approach, where would they be?

Joann gently tapped Mrs. Delarue on the arm. "It's so slow. Do you want to go home early?"

Mrs. Delarue smoothed her apron. "I am awfully tired today."

"But make sure to come back tomorrow," Joann chirped, then regretted her forced cheeriness. She'd do her level best to distract the woman tomorrow. And maybe the news would turn.

Please God. Let there be good news tomorrow. Protect all our boys.

If Joann ever had children, would she be like Mrs. Delarue, worry herself sick over them, or like her own mother, who'd walked away without a backward glance?

She shivered.

What if she didn't have maternal instincts? Not everyone did, and it seemed those who did suffered for it. Just look at Mrs. Delarue. Her pain was palpable, and Joann didn't know how she carried on. It must take a great deal of strength.

After Mrs. Delarue left, Joann took advantage of the slowdown to reduce the cash and get the checks out of the register. She filled the bank bag, intending to take it to the store's safe, but the register wouldn't close again. The old hunk of junk would be the death of her. Gritting her teeth, she banged the drawer shut. It sprang open, hitting her hip.

She yelped and rubbed the sore spot. "This fool register!"

"Here, let me." For the whisper of a second, Nathan placed his hands on Joann's waist and eased her aside.

She opened her mouth to protest, but his attention wasn't on her. It was on the machine, which made her feel wrong-footed and silly.

Leaving the cash drawer halfway pushed in, he lifted it a fraction, running his fingers over the sides of the register. His brow wrinkled in concentration.

"I'll be right back." He headed up the stairs.

Torn between staying put to guard the drawer, or forcing it shut so she could get on with work, Joann hesitated. No customers needed attention. She scooted a stool closer to the register and sat.

Nathan returned with a tiny screwdriver and a can of machine oil.

Joann surveyed the empty store. No doubt Nathan's orchard had more weeds than the store had customers right now. The homesickness for Barb she suffered was surely obvious to him, but she wasn't fragile. He should go tend his plants, not hang around babysitting a grumpy Jo. Guilt nipped at her.

She said, "You know, I can handle running the shop by myself after noon."

"I know."

"Cranky cash registers aside," Joann admitted. She drummed her fingers on the countertop. "Even this wouldn't be a problem if Dad would let me throw out the old thing."

"Nothing wrong with keeping it around. I can probably fix it."

He sounded like her father.

"What if I don't want it fixed?"

Nathan grunted. "Now you're just trying to pick a fight."

She wasn't picking a fight. She was trying to be considerate and respectful of his time.

Joann crossed her arms. Then, not wanting to appear confrontational, uncrossed them. "I appreciate you helping out, but I can manage until we hire on someone."

Nathan's expression clouded over, and he stopped fiddling with the register. She'd hurt him.

"Not that I don't want you here." She rushed on. "That's not it at all." She was doing this all wrong.

Nathan's expression didn't change.

Joann squirmed on the stool but held back from getting up and approaching him. Why couldn't he understand her need to handle the store on her own? And understand she cared about him enough to let him do his own thing? With other workers, every utterance from her mouth wasn't examined for hidden meaning. She could remind him of that, but she didn't.

Lamely, she said, "I don't want you neglecting the farm."

She meant she didn't want to tie him down, but to say so out loud? Not the time or place.

With a slow nod, he seemed to turn her words over in his mind. Maybe he didn't want to work at the store at all. Space away from each other during the workday might be a relief. Trustworthy and hardworking, Nathan was as dependable as the sunrise, but also tended to take over. If he kept hovering, she'd never find a new normal and learn how to manage without Barb.

Gingerly, he placed the screwdriver on the counter and spun it like a game of spin the bottle. "Joann, your dad already asked me to be here as much as I'm able. Offered a permanent job, if I wanted it."

Joann came off the stool, her shoes hitting the floor with a thump. "He what?"

Silence reared up between them, broken by a young boy approaching the register. He slid a pack of gum across the counter toward Nathan.

Nathan smiled at him. "This pretty lady will ring you up in a sec." He stepped aside. "Joann, you'd better take this." Turning on his heel, he strode away.

She fought the urge to call him back. She'd been left out again, but her gripe wasn't with him.

As she tended to the young customer, Nathan kept himself busy and out of her way, but he didn't leave.

Joann found her dad in the back office, sitting at the desk. A lamp gave extra light to the ledger he worked on. The sight of him calmly penciling tally marks fueled her frustration, but she kept her fidgety hands in her pockets.

"Dad, how could you consider hiring Nathan without talking to me first?" Her voice came out firm, if louder than intended.

Over the top of wire-framed readers, Dad met her gaze. Sighing, he closed the account book and placed the pencil on the book's brown cover. "I thought you were happy with the work he'd done with your little produce venture. Are you two on the outs?"

"No, we aren't on the outs."

Keep a level head.

She consciously willed the knot of muscles in her back to relax. It didn't work. "You have to admit, my *little* fresh produce venture has drawn in a steady stream of new regulars."

"Yes, it has." He nodded his agreement. "You and Nathan are a good team. He's been dependable and is a likable fellow. The customers take to him." He squinted at her. "Why don't you want him working in the store?"

"I didn't say I didn't want him working in the store."

Her dad leaned back in his chair and made a well-what-do-you-want-face worthy of a Red Skelton comedy act.

"It's just...," Joann spluttered. "Well, I'd like to talk over those kinds of decisions first." She stood ramrod straight.

"All right, then." Her dad scratched the back of his head and plucked at the tufts of hair at his nape. "What's your objection to Nathan working here?"

She could remind him Nathan had a farm to run but thought better of it. Stick to the point. Dad needed to hear her, loud and clear.

"I don't have an objection to Nathan working here. Not at all. I simply wanted to have a say."

"Well, I don't understand what the fuss is about," Dad grumbled. "You've never been a quiet one, and you said yourself you don't have an objection. Seems you're getting what you want." He opened the desk drawer, put the account book inside, closed the drawer, and turned the lock. Slipping the key into his shirt pocket, he frowned at her.

She was six years old again, reduced to a bothersome child making frivolous demands from her busy father. The desire to press her case and make him listen welled up in her and she tamped it down. No matter how tempting it was to stamp her feet or make a sassy remark, reacting like a child wouldn't advance her cause.

"Look, Jo. You needed help. With Barb married, I didn't want you to get overworked. Let me take care of you, why don't you? That's my job."

The sincerity and confusion plain on his features sapped all the fight right out of her. She nodded, though she didn't agree. Trying to drag him into the modern world exhausted her. Without a word, she returned to her post out front.

Later, Nathan approached her. "Are you mad at me?"

"Of course not." She snapped, then softened. "It was a miscommunication between me and Dad."

As soon as Nathan had had a conversation with Dad about working at the store, he could've talked it over with her as well. And he wanted to get married. Wasn't marriage a partnership? She stiffened her jaw. Well, at least she had confirmation her head was on straight. Blinking back furious tears, Joann found a cloth and polished first the counter, then the shelves, anything to avoid him.

"Are you sure you want me here?"

His plaintive tone stabbed at her. The truth was, she did, and she didn't.

"It's fine," she clipped out.

"That's a confidence booster."

"It's what Dad wants, and I'm sure we'll find plenty for you to do."

She'd deal with it.

As long as he didn't take over like the time he insisted on helping her paint the storage shed at school. He'd mixed green and yellow paint, then argued the color looked fine, right up until the whole football team lined up, pretending to wretch and gag. Joann and Nathan had been dubbed "Green Team" for the rest of eighth grade.

The need to assert herself came to the surface. She said, "You being here will suit me fine, but I can manage perfectly well on my own."

"I know you can."

All on its own, the old register sprang open and a shower of coins pinged onto the hardwood floor.

Joann refused to stop polishing shelves but couldn't help stealing a glance at Nathan.

He cocked an eyebrow. "You okay with me fixing that now?"

CHAPTER ELEVEN

Joann sipped water from her glass, then set it down on their table. The girls had met in Shreveport for lunch at a favorite spot, Murrell's.

Joann adjusted the collar of her shirt. July was really too warm for a mock turtleneck, even if it was thin knit and sleeveless. "I don't know why you bother with the menu, Barb. You always get the coleslaw and corn muffins."

"You never know." Barb scanned the menu. "One day I might surprise you."

A coughing fit overtook Joann, and she took another sip of water. "Speaking of surprises, when were you going to make an announcement? I don't want to let the news out accidentally." Pointedly, she stared at her sister's tummy. Anyone with eyes in their head could tell Barb had a bun in the oven.

Barb lowered her lashes and held the menu closer to her face. "Soon."

Time to change the subject.

Joann said, "I'm not sure what to do about Dad."

Barb put the menu down. "What about him?" She paled. "Is he having his spells again?"

Any big change might set Dad spiraling into a dark time, but that wasn't at all what Joann meant.

"No. At least I don't think so." She frowned. He'd been more tired than usual. A knot tightened between her shoulder blades. As soon as she got home, she'd schedule a doctor's appointment for him. Just to be sure.

Joann massaged her temples. How to put the problem she was having with Dad? She didn't want to guilt Barb for having a life, but since Barb had left, Dad treated Joann more like a temporary employee at the store. She settled on, "He said I didn't know how to run things, the house and stuff."

"What?" Barb laughed. "Did you burn his eggs or something?"

Joann batted her with a napkin. "I did not."

"What then?"

"Ever since he hired Nathan behind my back, I've felt left out."

Barb rolled her eyes. "What else is new?"

"I think he wants me to marry Nathan and..." She caught herself before saying anything about children. "I'm not keen on the idea right now." Before the conversation could veer off into a discussion about her and Nathan's history, she rushed on. "And there's another thing. Nathan is constantly looking over my shoulder at the store and he won't listen either."

Instead of demanding details, Barb wilted. "I know what you mean."

Joann's antennae shot up. She reached across the table for Barb's hand. "What is it?"

Wearing a watery smile, Barb slumped in her seat. "I miss that. You can read me. Don't get me wrong. Charles is wonderful, but he doesn't always understand."

"What doesn't he understand? You can tell me."

"He doesn't criticize, but he talks about his mother all the time." She hurried on. "That's not a bad thing. I love how much he loves his mother, but he keeps saying how much she'll love me, and how his mother loves to quilt, makes the best cakes, always had cookies for him after school. And then he says I'll be a perfect mom, exactly like his mother." An unhappy pall surrounded Barb as she moodily unfolded a napkin.

"I don't know if you'll be like his mother, but I agree you'll be a great mom." Joann added emphasis to her words. "I know it in my gut. And if he's not complaining, you must be doing things right."

"There's something else." Barb bit her lip and lowered her eyelashes. "It's so silly. Crammed into the apartment with his roommate, I can barely function. Charles's buddies are always around, and they're all gung ho about his birthday, talking about a party at the apartment." Barb clasped her forehead. "I can't deal with it."

"Doesn't he see how hard it is for you?" Joann scowled. "Being pregnant, not to mention crammed into a tiny apartment and adjusting to a new city, is enough to deal with. A birthday party?"

"I tried to tell him how tired I am all the time, but he keeps saying his friends will help." Her lips puckered like she'd sucked a dill pickle. "Like those guys are any use. And every time they light up smokes, I get nauseated and have to dash for the bathroom."

Joann chewed the inside of her cheek, barely stopping herself from insisting Barb come home. She'd met the roommate, Jerry. A nice guy, but sharing an apartment clearly wasn't working, temporary or not. For Barb, anyway.

Joann said, "When is Jerry moving out?"

"Not for weeks, and I wanted to make Charles a fancy birthday dinner!" Barb wailed. Loudly.

Joann's eyes popped open in alarm, and she shushed her sister. Other customers stared. Shoulders lifted in a helpless gesture, she smiled at them and patted Barb's hand.

She whispered into Barb's ear. "Do you need to go outside for a breath of air or go to the restroom?"

The waitress came over. "Is she all right?"

Joann nodded. "Yes, yes. Sorry."

Instead of leaving, the waitress stood at the table, drawing the attention of every last person in the place.

Joann soothed, "Hey, Barb. Don't worry. Bring his mom's cookbook to me. You and I will make the dinner together at the house. His birthday can be a family celebration. Put off his friends if you want. Let Charles do a night out with his buddies later." She gabbled on. "You could tell Dad about the baby. That would make him happy."

"I'm sorry." Barb flattened her palm against her stomach. "I'm so emotional these days." With a pitiful expression, she turned sad, waiflike eyes on the waitress.

The look had never worked on Joann before, but it did now. She couldn't blame her sister.

The waitress smiled, showing a gap between her front teeth. "Don't think a thing about it, hon." She winked at Joann.

Here Joann had thought Barb could help her figure out a way to manage Dad and Nathan, and instead she'd promised to help Barb plan a birthday party.

CHAPTER TWELVE

Newspaper in hand, Dad sat heavily in the wooden chair and gazed through the store's front window, focusing on nothing. "I don't understand what's going on in the world these days." He dropped the paper. The newsprint folded in on itself, hiding headlines about the Watts riots in Los Angeles. Thirty-five dead, four thousand arrested, and forty million in damages, numbers Joann couldn't fathom. A week before, President Johnson had signed The Voting Rights Act prohibiting voter discrimination, a step in the right direction, but America was groaning under pressures from every side. The Vietnam conflict screamed from the headlines every day.

Dad blinked blearily. If Barb were here, she could cheer him with a silly joke or by bringing him a flower. Joann had never been one for such things.

She stood awkwardly by the newspaper rack. "Want some more coffee, Dad?"

"No, that's all right."

"The fellows will be in soon." Joann bustled about, checking the coffee station and arranging the cups.

"Honey, I think I might need to do some things at the house today."

Joann watched him shuffle toward the back.

She knew that later, when she had a break after lunchtime, she'd return home to find his bedroom door shut. If she peeked in, the room would be dark, window shades drawn.

He stopped walking away, but kept his back to her. "I'm glad Nathan will be here soon to help you."

Was that the real reason he'd hired Nathan? Had he felt the sadness coming on? It was impossible to know what circumstances sent Dad to bed with exhaustion.

As soon as the sound of his footsteps faded, Joann went to the phonebook and found Dr. Gill's number, although she knew what he'd say after the exam and a few tests. Rest and nutrition for Dad, and for Joann to demonstrate patience.

The next afternoon, after her prediction about the doctor visit played out exactly as she'd expected, Joann sat at the kitchen table, flipping through the cookbook and attempting a meal plan. The birthday bash was only a few days away. Barb had called with a list of Charles's favorite foods, and a list of excuses for the girls' planning session. Her morning sickness had not only continued but kicked into high gear, progressing into afternoon and evening sickness.

Joann picked at the seam of her shirt hem. Barb should be feeling better by now. Maybe she should insist her sister see a doctor off-base. It wasn't her business, but if Barb didn't improve soon, she'd put her oar in.

Careful with the cookbook so dear to Charles's family, she paged through it a second time, reading the inscriptions of past cooks, and stopped at a Robert Frost quote.

We love the things we love for what they are.

The quote repeated in her head. We love the things we love for what they are. Her mind added, or *who they are.*

Nathan.

She did love him for who he was. That's why they got along so well. The curtains over the sink fluttered in a playful breeze, seeming to agree.

But what if Nathan had changed? Really was ready to be more serious? If he decided to push the topic, she'd have to explain. She couldn't give up the store to be a farm wife. The Nathan she knew wouldn't take that well. Then what?

A sharp rap sounded at the back door and Nathan stuck his head in. "Hey, Jo."

She nearly dropped the book. Instead, she set it on the table, closed it, and lifted her hands away as if, at any moment, the book might burst open and start to talk.

Oblivious to her reaction, Nathan hung on the doorframe, half in and half out. "There's a lady at the store to pick up shoes she special ordered?"

Joann blinked. This August heat and her woolgathering ways had dulled her wits. That's all it was. "I'll be right there."

Before leaving the house, Joann pressed an ear to Dad's door. No sound. Perhaps he'd only been run-down and tired. Perhaps a day or two of rest would set him right. In silent prayer, she brought her steepled fingers to her lips.

Please God, help my dad.

More eloquent words failed her, but she trusted the Great Physician to do His work.

She spent an hour in the store, then came back to the silent house. In the kitchen, a dirty plate held the crust of a sandwich, a sign Dad had eaten.

Her mood lifted. She started a list for the upcoming party, but didn't dare leave Dad on his own for long.

Like a trolley stuck on a short route, she trod back and forth across the road from house to store and back again.

Until she found Dad at the kitchen table, his hair disheveled and pajamas rumpled.

Joann took a chair next to him. "How are you feeling?" Her gaze lit on the glass of water in front of him. "Can I get you anything? Ice? A straw?"

"Jo, go on over to the store and stay there until it closes."

Joann flushed hot. "I'm sorry, Dad. Did I make too much noise? I didn't mean to disturb you."

He sighed, a tired sound. Joann would rather hear his grousing.

He patted her on the arm. "You're not disturbing me, but you're going to wear a dip in the road." He rubbed bleary eyes. "Don't fret so much, hon. I need a rest, is all. Be right as rain tomorrow."

Sadness visited with no rhyme or reason, and it stayed as long as it liked. No amount of willpower, sleep, or wishing would evict it before it ran its course. Maybe he would feel better tomorrow.

"All right, I'll go." She kissed the top of his head. "I'll fix you a glass of cornbread and milk first, though."

She found a glass and made the snack, setting it in front of him before taking one last trip across the road. No matter how much she brooded, she wouldn't come home until the store closed.

At the day's end, Joann collected the receipts, cleared the cash drawer, and headed to the back office.

Nathan was mopping a spill near the soda cooler and spoke as she walked by. "Cash register give you any more trouble?"

Joann shook her head. She should thank him for fixing it but couldn't bring herself to. Defeat wasn't in her nature.

"Hey," he called after her. "Mind if I switch the music?"

The background of KWKH's country music hadn't registered with her. It was the soundtrack of her childhood: Elvis, Hank Williams, and Patsy Cline, along with others from The Louisiana Hayride.

Her dad's music.

Nostalgia poked at her. A change would be good. "Sure."

A grumpy sadness plagued her as she balanced accounts and checked sales to see what needed restocking before they could call it done. With all her hopping back and forth, she'd barely been in the store, but had exhausted herself all the same.

Music blared through the store. What was he thinking, having it so loud? Joann shoved back from the desk and strode to the open door. She took a step into the hall and smack into Nathan's broad chest.

"Whoa, there!" He grasped her elbows and steadied her. "I was coming to find you." He let her go but didn't step back. "Are you okay?"

"Yes. Didn't see you there, that's all." Joann made a show of brushing off her blouse. She'd completely forgotten to put on a shop apron today.

"No. I mean, are you really okay? You're taking care of your dad, planning a birthday party, and watching the store." He bent down to meet her eyes. "You had to keep watch over me as well. Have to make sure I don't give someone a cabbage when they ask for a turnip, or burn down the store."

Joann flushed at his gentle teasing.

"I'm here for you, Jo. Always."

She knew that. During rocky times, Nathan had been there when it counted, just not always in the way she needed him.

His comfort drew her as surely as the moon pulled the tides.

If only she could trust him not to rush a change in their relationship. He'd said he'd wait, and she could use an uncomplicated friendship right now.

Resisting the urge to melt into him, she said, "The music's too loud."

He cocked his head to the side. "Is it? Do you think your dad can hear it?" Concern creased his brow, and he turned around, ready to go change the volume.

Which wasn't loud at all.

She was being crabby.

She touched his back. "Not really."

"Good." He faced her, revealing a wicked grin. "Because I picked the song especially for you."

Listening to the lyrics, Joann narrowed her eyes as "It's My Party" floated through the air.

Nathan shifted on his feet, ready to dart away, a move he'd perfected on the sisters during his joke-playing days. "It's the perfect party song, yeah? Fits your mood too."

Her mouth puckered but laughter tickled her throat, making it impossible to scowl longer than a second.

"Nathan Poole, you are incorrigible."

She shoved him, and he pretended to stagger back.

"Made you laugh."

"Come on, let's finish up."

The record stopped. During the break, Nathan took Joann's hand. "Tell me about the birthday party."

So she talked about the party, relaxing as he teased and bossed her about what celebratory snacks they should have as they straightened the store in preparation for the next day. Nathan had stacked the record player for continuous music, and pop songs lightened her mood. Or maybe it was Nathan. After a while, she invited him to Charles's birthday. It seemed wrong not to.

Another song came on.

Nathan handed her a price label to put on a shelf of school supplies. "Have you sold many records?"

Joann shook her head. "I didn't mean for Dad to set everything up without my input." Another thing she'd wanted to discuss beforehand. What was it with Dad plowing ahead without talking over details? Now, because she'd been the one to put a bee in his bonnet, she had to take the results. "It might not have been a good idea. After all, people could go to a record shop in a city. We're not a great distance from Shreveport, and we can't compete with a specialty store like Stan's." She grimaced. "Please don't tell Dad I said so."

"Cross my heart." He pantomimed drawing an X on his chest. "But business might pick up."

"Did anyone buy a record while I was out?"

"No. But new ideas are what keep businesses thriving. Don't be so hard on yourself."

Joann laid her cool fingertips across her burning eyelids.

"Hey." Nathan grasped her wrists, uncovering her face. "For what it's worth, I think your ideas are great. You're always looking for ways to make everything better. You make everything better."

Unspoken words hung in the air, but fear kept her from demanding an explanation of his last comment. He kissed the inside of her left wrist, sending sparks of pleasure along her nerve endings. She shuddered and drew away. Better to end the evening as it was.

"I think we can lock up shop. We're done."

Never breaking eye contact with her, Nathan nodded. "For now." He cast a glance upward. "Except for the music. Let's stay for this last song." He gripped her fingers. "Besides, I need to practice my dancing for the party, right?"

"There won't be any dancing."

"Okay then. Let's just say you owe me for staying late."

He had her laughing again as he wriggled his body, snapped his fingers, and strutted around her.

"You look like a demented rooster."

"You're going to pay for that!"

He grabbed her and spun her around to the melody of "Just One Look" until she begged for mercy. Pulling her close, he smiled. She leaned into his chest and closed her eyes as he buried his face in her hair.

They slowed to a sway, comfortable with each other in the way of old, trusted friends and safe places. She breathed in the faint smell of wood smoke and soap, trying to ignore the lyrics to the song.

CHAPTER THIRTEEN

To Joann's relief, Dad returned to his normal duties the next day. His steps were slow, but he did his typical tasks, looking over the stock and greeting customers—if with less enthusiasm than usual.

He ran a finger across a top shelf and wiped the dust on his apron. "Isn't it time for a good cleaning?"

"Yes. I was planning to get to it soon." Joann was well aware of the need for a deep clean.

The wedding and general busyness had taken up her time. Now back-to-school season was upon them. She'd planned to get to it in mid-September.

"Do you suppose you and Mrs. Delarue could scrub up the place? And ask Nathan to pitch in. Or call in one of the high school boys."

"I will."

It wasn't worth telling him she had it on the schedule. At least he suggested the part-time workers help out. She'd been at him for a year to let others do more of the heavy lifting, but found no joy in his acquiescence.

His color was off, washed out, and he carried himself cautiously. A strong wind might come along any minute and blow him over.

She said, "If you'll watch the register, I'll call around and see who's available."

"That's fine." Dad put on a fresh pot of coffee and reached for a newspaper, keeping to his routine, even though the early morning customers had come and gone long ago.

Joann headed to the back office.

After she'd called Mrs. Delarue and a couple of their high school workers, Joann rolled up her sleeves and set to work organizing what she could between customers until help arrived.

She wouldn't bother Nathan. The farm wouldn't run itself, scaled down or not. Plants and the soil always needed attention, not to mention general farm upkeep.

She'd handle things without him.

Two boys arrived, one after the other. She waved a list at them. "Here, take this. But before you start on it, move the shelving from the corner to the front area by the sewing supplies. No goofing off." She gave them the eye. She meant business today.

While Joann waited for Mrs. Delarue to arrive, she tended to customers. The whole time she itched to get cleaning. Sooner started, sooner done. She felt caught out, letting the cleaning get away from her, never mind she had good reasons. Excuses were only that. Excuses.

Between dealing with customers, she straightened an endcap display and rearranged sections, dusting as she went. Joann's spirits lifted. There was something about freshening up a place. It did the heart good to see a thing renewed.

An hour later, a flustered Mrs. Delarue arrived. "I came as soon as I could."

Joann slid a loaf of bread onto the depleted shelf. "I appreciate it. Watch the register. I'll check back in an hour or so." Joann tied a handkerchief over her hair and knotted it at the nape of her neck. "But come upstairs and find me if you need me."

If it made Dad happy, she'd banish every last cobweb and dust bunny before the day was out.

She wrestled the mop bucket up the stairs and set to it, but had only finished half the floor before Mrs. Delarue interrupted her. Behind her came Mary Weaver, a thirteen-year-old, freckle-faced waif, a girl so shy she barely said more than three words during any given encounter.

Exasperated, Mrs. Delarue crossed her arms. "She won't tell me what she wants and insists on speaking with you."

The girl stood as if she didn't want to take up any room, arms tight against her sides, bony knees touching.

Joann smiled at Mary. "It's all right, Mrs. Delarue. I've got it."

Mrs. Delarue sighed, turned, and plodded back downstairs.

With the back of one wrist, Joann wiped her sweaty forehead. "What is it, Mary?"

The girl sidled up to Joann and whispered, "My friend has come to visit."

Joann understood. The girl had gotten her period and didn't want anyone else to ring up the purchase. Mary flushed, making her freckles stand out.

Joann well remembered the agony of similar situations and pitched her voice low. "There's no need to be embarrassed, Mary. I'll go get what you need and ring it up for you, all right?"

They went to the proper aisle where Joann discreetly put the requested items in a paper bag. While Joann was at the register ringing up Mary's purchase, she caught sight of Dad schmoozing with a fellow in a suit. The pair meandered around the store, stopping here and there. The man didn't pick up so much as a can of corn. Definitely not a customer.

What was Dad up to?

Joann strained to catch the conversation, to no avail. Probably an expansion or remodel. Her jaw tightened. Had Dad left her out again?

She locked eyes with him, but his gaze skittered away like a kid caught stealing bubblegum. Ratcheting up his friendly demeanor toward the man, he gestured to another section, and they moved on. Away from her.

If she could twitch her nose and magically listen in on the conversation, she'd do it in a heartbeat.

Joann flagged down Mrs. Delarue and put her on the register. "If you need help and you can't get Dad's attention, send one of the boys to get me."

If she sidled up to Dad and the man, she'd surely look the fool, and get the bum's rush, to boot.

She went upstairs, scooted her mop bucket to an advantageous position, and watched Dad from above.

Maybe the gentleman was a banker and Dad wanted to make a good impression. It would explain Dad's sudden interest in cleaning the store.

Dad and the man left together, leaving Joann to stew. When he came back, he was a moving target, disappearing altogether after sending one of the young helpers with a message saying he'd be back later.

Six o'clock came and went.

At twenty after, he breezed by her as she wiped up a milk spill near the coolers.

"Going to look at the books." He quick-stepped down the aisle.

"Can we talk a minute?" Joann dropped a handful of saturated paper towels into a nearby trashcan.

Dad didn't break his stride. "At dinner."

Oh no. She wasn't going to be put off. Joann hurriedly wiped up the rest of the spill with a damp rag and trailed after Dad.

A closed office door greeted her. She rapped sharply and opened it without waiting for a response. Dad sat at his desk, an open ledger in front of him, the picture of industry.

Or avoidance.

"Dad, what was the tour you gave the fellow in the suit all about?"

He peered at her over glasses. "Let me finish up before we talk." He licked his pencil and scrutinized the ledger.

"I'd rather you told me now."

Grasping the pencil on either end with his forefingers, he set it down just so, as if it were a stick of dynamite. "I wanted to check over the finances before I said anything to you."

Joann dragged a chair to sit opposite him. "Are we in trouble?" Couldn't be. She'd recently examined the books herself. All was in the black.

"No. Nothing like that."

Joann laid her hand on her chest. "Then what?"

"Mr. Brumble is interested in the store."

Joann's brow wrinkled. "Interested?"

"Storekeeping is hard work. I know my episodes have shifted the burden to you, and Barb isn't around to help anymore. I don't like it."

"Oh, Dad. Don't worry about me. Haven't I always managed?"

"I still don't like it. What if I got sick and you had to do it all? It's too much." He firmed his jaw. "Mr. Brumble is looking to buy a grocery store."

The bottom fell out of Joann's stomach. She might be sick. "You can't, Dad! Our family has owned this store for generations."

"That's not a good enough reason to hang on to it."

"What about our heritage? The community you're always on about?"

Dad took off his glasses and set them down, then placed both fists on the desk. "If it came to it and I couldn't keep up, I'd rather sell it than see it run into the ground."

Joann's mouth dropped open. "Run into the ground? You think I'd run it into the ground? How could you say such a thing? I've been doing every job you've given me for years, Dad. Years."

"I know, but you always had help before." He pinched the bridge of his nose. "You're a hard worker, but I'm not sure you have business sense. Take your idea of selling records. How many have we sold?"

"That's not fair! I said I wanted to talk about it, but you went on and bought records without me."

Dad frowned. "Besides having business smarts, a store owner has to take responsibility. Why bring an idea to the table if you weren't committed? Sounds like backtracking to me."

Her mind scrambled for an argument with firm footing. A move left or right and she'd slip into the hole opening up beneath her.

"The produce display brought sales."

"But you can't invest in hit-or-miss ideas."

"Dad, you can't sell the store!"

"Don't worry. If I sold to anyone, they'd have to guarantee you a job as long as you need it."

"I want more than a job. I want the store."

"This conversation is getting out of hand. I thought this would take the burden off you. I've seen you struggling since Barb left. If you're serious, and if you get married and he wants to be a store owner, then I'll be happy to keep it in the family."

Only if she married? He still didn't think she could manage the business on her own, that she needed a man to run the show.

Joann clenched her jaw so tight her ears popped.

Well. She'd just have to prove him wrong.

CHAPTER FOURTEEN

The day's heat held well past dark. Joann tossed and turned late into the night.

Sell the store? Dad couldn't be serious.

She rubbed her stuffy nose. Her head ached, chasing away sleep. With a huff, she sat up and flipped her pillow to the cool side. She laid flat on her back. It was no use.

A bit of light came through the window, almost illuminating the outline of an old water stain on the ceiling. Even in good light, the stain was indistinct, but she knew it was there. Always had been.

She blinked at it.

Why did everyone in her life have to stir the pot? First Barb falling in love with a man who'd take her away from the area, then Nathan coming home from college and suggesting he might want a different level of relationship, and now Dad ignoring all the years he'd trained Joann to run the store.

She'd been perfectly content before they'd gone and changed on her.

Joann frowned. She had to admit Dad had, at least in part, a valid point about her inexperience and lack of business sense. Barb, not Joann, had been the one to take business classes. The one good at numbers.

Joann sighed. Regardless of the facts stacked against her, she couldn't imagine a life without the store. She cared for the community by providing the peoples' needs, whether it be milk, medicine, advice, or encouragement. There was nothing else she'd rather spend her time on.

She should've spoken up about the records when Dad surprised her at Barb's reception. Or any number of times when he'd pushed ahead or ignored her.

Half her troubles came from staying quiet at key moments.

Joann threw off the sweat-dampened sheet and padded downstairs for an aspirin and a cold bottle of Coke to wash it down.

Not bothering with the lights, she got a Coke from the Frigidaire and popped the cap off. Released carbonation hissed in the quiet.

What was she going to do?

In all thy ways acknowledge Him.

This time, the verses from Proverbs didn't come with a guilt trip. The admonition to trust God instead of struggling to figure it out on her own felt more like a lifeline.

She served the community the best way she knew how, in a way her gifts suited. That couldn't be wrong. Even if she married Nathan, she'd never ask him to give up his farm to run the store. Dad would have to see. Getting married simply to satisfy some old-fashioned notions was the wrong reason for anyone to marry.

Joann wanted more.

She prayed, and as she did, a direction came to her.

The next morning, she took special care with her hair and makeup. Barb's old textbooks sat on Joann's bedside table, along with the notes she'd taken after she'd prayed over her situation and before she'd finally succumbed to sleep for a few hours.

As soon as Dad left for the store, she called Barb. On the third ring, the roommate, Jerry, answered and Joann asked for Barb.

"What is it?" Barb said, her voice groggy.

"Are you feeling any better?" Joann twisted the yellow telephone cord around her wrist. The impulse to unload about her conversation with Dad surged inside her, but she held back. Her sister didn't need another burden right now.

Barb groaned. "Please don't say you can't do the party at the house."

"It's not that. I've got it under control." A harmless white lie. Joann made a mental note to organize the food. And decorations. "I want to learn more about business and have been studying your old books."

"You're welcome to them."

"Thanks, but I might need a bit more. Do me a favor. If you think of anyone I can talk to about running a business, let me know."

"Is something going on I should worry about?" A note of alarm crept into Barb's tone.

"Of course not. The only thing you need to worry about is not upchucking at the birthday party."

"Tell me about it. The worst is the car ride."

They talked for a while about the party before hanging up.

The conversation reminded her of something. Dad hadn't considered how Barb would react to him selling the store, either.

***

On Charles's birthday, all day long the attic fan circulated air through the house. They planned for a late celebration dinner after the heat abated, but if a scorcher made an appearance, the store had air conditioning. They could go over and listen to the radio while cooling off.

Barb and Joann stood on the porch. The men clustered around Charles's car, likely discussing the mystery of the vehicle's innards.

"Should we go in?" Joann asked Barb.

"Probably." Barb stirred up a small current of air with a church hand fan, the depiction of Jesus a blur as she flapped away. Face scarlet, she scraped her hair back. The ends had lost their usual flip, if they'd had any to begin with. "We should tell the men to come on. If we leave them to it, they'll stay out here all evening. The food will get cold."

As if hearing his wife, Charles spoke to Nathan and Dad, prompting the three to head toward the door.

A sweaty Barb relaxed. "Thank goodness." She lowered her voice and placed a hand on her stomach. "I'm so ready to get this over with."

Joann knew her sister didn't mean the birthday dinner.

Under the empire-waist dress, the swell of Barb's stomach couldn't be ignored, but Dad hadn't seemed to notice. He'd perked up at the idea of Barb coming. Then, when she arrived, he'd barely given her a passing hello and a peck on the cheek before glomming on to Charles.

Joann followed Barb in, and they began ferrying the food to the dining room.

"Here, Barb," Joann handed over a casserole dish of stir-fried beef and peppers nestled on a bed of rice.

Red and blue crepe paper streamers hung from the walls, stock left over from the fourth of July, a fact no one had to know. Blue and silver paper cutout letters wished Charles a happy birthday. A vase holding wild sunflowers from the back yard sat on the table, completing the decorations.

Joann placed another dish on the table. "I hope Charles likes bacon in his green beans. Do they do that where he's from?"

"I'm sure." A flustered Barb smoothed her dress. Two spots of color flamed her cheeks, and even her neck turned red.

Joann asked, "Should I get you a cool cloth? Are you feeling quite well yet?"

"Not really. I'd rather put off telling Dad about the baby, but Charles said we should share the news tonight."

Resentment toward Charles spurted inside Joann, even though she agreed with the need for an announcement soon. What was wrong with her? He was Barb's husband, and she was a wife now, no longer just Joann's sister.

Joann picked a stray leaf from the table and flicked it away. "That's probably best. Go fetch in the cake, would you?"

Joann had baked another white cake, but this time topped it with whipped cream and cherries. An easy cherry torte would've taken less time, but everyone deserved their favorite for their birthday. Doubly so for Charles, since he was, after all, family.

The men came in and Barb joined Charles, cleaving to him as if he were a life raft on a stormy sea. Her eyes stayed fixed on his when she said, "We have something to tell you all."

Smiling with the peace of the untroubled, Charles tucked Barb's hand into the crook of his elbow and ducked his head.

Barb blurted, "We're having a baby."

Dad gave a tiny start like he'd been goosed, then beamed as he spared the slightest of glances to Barb's belly.

No narrowing of the eyes, no suspicious look. Joann let out her breath.

Dad approached the couple with a calm and steady gait, kissed Barb's cheek, and clapped Charles on the back. "I couldn't be happier."

His subdued behavior gave Joann pause, but if she had to name the emotion flowing from her father, she'd call it gentle pride.

"Congratulations!" Nathan entered the circle and hugged Barb, tossing Joann a questioning look.

It wasn't difficult to count the weeks between a rushed wedding and a baby announcement. Joann felt like hiding her face from Nathan, but she stiffened her spine instead. The question in his eyes shifted to knowing and his expression shuttered.

He released Barb. "We better let you sit down!"

She waved him off. "Don't start. I'm perfectly able."

Nathan clasped Charles on the side of his neck. "Congratulations!"

The sentiment rolled out too heartily.

Nathan didn't let go right away. Instead, the two younger men locked eyes. After a beat, Charles nodded.

Dad ignored the tense, silent exchange. "Well, I guess this is a double celebration, then." Stretching to his full height, he puffed out his chest. The apples of his cheeks pinked and his eyes crinkled in pleasure.

Joann almost believed he hadn't known.

CHAPTER FIFTEEN

With dusk, cooler air came through the open windows. The meal progressed. Easy conversation flowed around the table, the men engaging in light banter, sparking none of the dreaded fireworks, thankfully, and she liked to see Dad enjoying Charles and Nathan's company.

They would be all right.

She tapped Barb on the arm. "Help me clear?"

"Sure."

The rumble of male voices drifted into the kitchen, competing with the clink of dishes and running water.

Barb opened the top drawer and fished out a clean dishtowel. "You wash and I'll dry."

The apprehension of the last few weeks left Joann faint, but she'd never say so. Neither did she ask Barb if her physical ailments troubled her, although after the cleanup, Barb suggested they all play the board game Joann had given Charles, so it seemed she had perked up.

Dad nudged Charles. "You're about to realize how competitive Barb can be."

"I guess so." Charles draped an arm across Barb's shoulders as she playfully wrinkled her nose at Dad.

She passed Charles the sheet of game instructions. "Don't listen to him." She turned to the group, cupped her mouth, and stage whispered, "Don't give away my strategy."

Charles was concentrating on the directions when he said, in a tone of complete seriousness, "I'll always let you win. After all, you're the best prize any guy could ask for."

It was the longest sentence he'd uttered in Joann's presence, and so sweet. Romantic, even. She, Dad, and Nathan stared at him.

Sensing the gawping eyes, Charles looked up and awareness dawned on his features. A wash of red spread from his neck to ears.

Dad broke the silence. "Good man."

Nathan said, "Smart man."

They all laughed, Charles included.

As the game moved along, Joann made popcorn and put an LP on the stereo. Loud chatter filled the house. Nathan and Barb were the best players, reverting to acting as if they were twelve and eleven again. Barb flipped alliances between Dad and Nathan, depending on who was winning at the moment.

The comforting coziness of older days returned. Ever since Barb had announced her hurried plans to marry Charles, Joann had been afraid her sister had made a terrible mistake, but from all appearances Barb had her husband in hand. The worry knots binding Joann's heart loosened.

Joann gave up her last card. "I'm out." She put her game piece into the box. "Anyone want coffee?"

A chorus of yeses rose from the table, and she went to the kitchen and put on the electric percolator. Soon the aroma of the fresh brew filled the house, along with the laughter of her family. And Nathan.

If only such moments could be captured like fireflies and kept safe in a jar.

She took a tray to the dining room and served everyone, then poured herself a cup. "I'm going to sit on the porch while Barb finishes slaughtering you guys."

"I'm not giving up yet." Nathan hunched over the board, the tip of his tongue peeking from the corner of his mouth.

"Some people never learn." Joann shook her head and headed outside.

Sipping her coffee, she watched the road. Every once in a while, a car's headlights cut into the dark as it went by. A crescent moon hung in a hazy sky. The food and company had done her good. Slipping off her shoes, she sat on the swing and set it in motion.

The creak of the front door sounded in harmony with the night sounds of conversation drifting from the house and the yard crickets.

"Hey, Joann." Charles's voice floated out into the warm night as naturally as if he belonged.

"Hey."

"You mind?" He held up his pack of cigarettes.

She didn't care for cigarettes, but neither did she want to be rude. No doubt his nerves had been tested tonight.

She said, "Go ahead."

A match flame illuminated his face as he lit his cigarette. The crinkle on his inhale indicated a hard draw. "Barb won't let me smoke around her. Says it makes her sick to her stomach." He took another deep drag. "I'm going to give it up."

Joann took the last sip of her coffee only to find the liquid lukewarm. She must've been outside longer than she realized.

He said, "You know, Barb thinks you walk on water."

"Does she?" Joann heard the smugness in her voice. Lazily, she put out a stocking-clad toe and gave the swing a small push to keep it going.

"Yes, ma'am. You're a tough act to follow."

Joann couldn't tell, but thought his serious tone might camouflage a smidgen of humor.

He walked to the edge of the porch and flicked ash into the grass. "You ever heard of Stellar Records?"

Abruptly, Joann sat up, stopping the swing's motion. "In Shreveport?"

Stellar was owned by a woman, and women business owners were few and far between.

Charles pointed at her. "Bingo. Anyway, Jerry has a buddy who made a record there."

A connection. From none other than the friendly, but troublesome, roommate, Jerry. Bless him.

"Is the musician anyone I would know?"

"Nah." He coughed. "Well, Barb told me to get the lady's number for you. The lady who owns the studio. In case you wanted to call." He went down the front steps and stubbed out his cigarette in the dirt. Reaching into his pocket, he retrieved a card and extended it toward her. "Barb says you are smart at business, but she thought this lady might have some encouraging words for you. Advice and whatnot. And it's music. Anyway, Barb said to give this to you."

The suggestion touched her right in the center of her being. Her sister hadn't forgotten all about her. Indeed, this was proof she had faith in Joann's capabilities.

Like cool water poured onto dry earth, she soaked it up.

Joann took the card and studied the number.

"Give her a call. Maybe meet up with her. I can go with you if you want. And Barb too, of course."

"Why, thank you, Charles." Joann blinked back tears. The support of family meant everything. "What a kind gesture."

Charles shuffled awkwardly, as if his feet had grown two sizes in the last minutes and now they wouldn't cooperate. "I suppose I should go back in." He lingered.

Joann suspected he was working up his courage to tackle another round of overeager competition. Or perhaps he simply preferred the quiet.

She said, "Let's stay outside a few minutes. It's nice."

Charles lifted his face to the dark sky. "It is."

"I wanted to ask you something anyway." She sensed rather than saw him tense. "About the cookbook. Is it all right if I add a few notes in it for Barb? I think she'd like that."

He almost laughed. "Oh. Sure."

"It'll be a surprise."

"Sounds fine to me. I won't tell."

They lingered on the front porch in companionable silence for another ten minutes or so before heading in.

After everyone left, Joann tucked the card in the corner of her vanity mirror. Several gospel singers in the area had recorded there. Stellar Records catered to anyone who wanted to make a record and had the cash. Her heart picked up its tempo. She read the print, Patty Hightower, owner. Perhaps she would find time to talk with Joann.

***

Why she put off calling the number, Joann couldn't say. For two mornings, the card remained in plain view, in the corner of the mirror. She couldn't miss it, but still hadn't picked up the phone.

As she got ready for work, removing her big curlers, her eyes drifted to the small print of Miss Hightower's number.

"Ouch!"

A knot of hair drifted loose and she rubbed at a spot near her crown. In her distraction, she'd ripped hair right out of her head. She dropped the comb and snatched up the card. Fine. She'd call today. Scowling at her reflection, she stuck out her tongue, then set the card on the vanity top and once again took up the brush to fix her hair.

Ten minutes later, she opened the back door of the store. It creaked and she worked the hinge. She needed to oil it.

She sighed. The hinge could wait. The squeak wasn't anything new. She headed to the area near the front.

Dad puttered around, bringing in papers for the inside rack. Unaware of her presence, he bent and straightened the doormat.

Right as rain, just like he'd said, more or less. He had a pallor. She'd keep an eye on him. Sneak in extra vitamins.

She didn't want him to catch her hovering, so set to work.

In between customers, she unpacked boxes of Crayolas, school paste, and Big Chief tablets.

She grabbed a blank poster and markers to draw a sign advertising the school supplies. The bell over the door chimed and three teenage girls burst in, giggling, making a beeline for the hair products.

Joann said, "Dad, can you watch the register?" She didn't need his help but wanted him nearby to talk with him. She'd made up her mind to call Stellar Records today, and if the day dribbled away before she got to it, her courage might well dribble away as well.

Dad pulled up a stool. "Too bad Nathan isn't in today."

The stroke of her marker hesitated, producing a blobby mark on the poster. She covered the mistake by changing the style of the letters and carried on. "We do all right." With a few more creative slashes, she finished and capped the marker. "I was wondering if I could have the afternoon off one of those days Nathan comes in."

"I guess so. What for?"

With a different color marker, Joann drew a wavy-lined border on the sign. "Barb suggested I go speak with a businesswoman in Shreveport." Inwardly, Joann cringed at hiding behind her sister's skirts. Had she always been so dependent on Barb to back her up? She'd have to learn to stand on her own. Or get Dad on her side.

"A businesswoman, you say?" Dad frowned. "What kind of business?"

"She runs a recording studio."

Dad harrumphed, crossing his arms over the top of his belly.

Joann pretended to study the sign. The giggling girls carried an assortment of barrettes and hair products to the checkout. Dad straightened, a model friendly proprietor, as he rang up their purchases.

After the girls left, his grumpiness reappeared. "Where's this recording studio at?"

"Shreveport." Joann bit her lip, expecting Dad to launch into excuses or go silent again.

"Since Barb has put her oar in, maybe you two should ask Charles about it before you go over there."

Joann ducked her head to hide a smile. "Charles was the one who gave me the phone number. It actually came about through one of his friends."

"Oh." Dad ran a hand along his jaw. "That's all right, then."

Of course it was, if Charles said so. Joann held back a sigh. At least she'd achieved part of her goal. One day, Dad would see her worth.

There was more than one way to skin a cat.

She put the finished sale sign in the front window and went straight to the phone to set up an appointment with Miss Hightower.

CHAPTER SIXTEEN

Joann knocked a box of Astro Pops off the candy display and caught it before they all went flying, but four of the suckers had gotten loose. She picked up the multicolored lollipops and jammed them into the cardboard holder, then promptly upended the SweeTarts, sending a slew of rolls spinning across the floor.

Take a breath. Slow down.

Today she'd meet with Miss Patty Hightower. Too bad it couldn't have been earlier in the day. She hadn't slept a wink, had compensated with too much coffee, and now she was jittery on top of being tired.

Dad came over to help and bent down.

"I'll get it." Joann reached under the candy cabinet and did an arm sweep, gathering the wayward SweeTarts. They weren't even dusty, thanks to the recent deep clean of the store, which made her unaccountably grateful.

Dad rearranged the candy display, tipping his head forward with his father-knows-best look. "I can tell you're nervous. Take Nathan with you. He'll be on hand if you have car trouble or get lost."

"I've been driving to Shreveport for years."

Truthfully, the temptation to ask Nathan along was hard to resist. She hated driving in the city, but she had to learn to do things on her own.

"You always had Barb along before."

"Like she could help with car trouble."

The flesh under Dad's chin wobbled. He lowered his voice. "Why do you have to be so hardheaded?"

Last year, she'd have told him it must be inherited, but the encroaching gray in the little hair he had left and the fatigue he hadn't been able to shake stopped her. She'd rather have her stubborn Dad back than win an argument because he'd run out of steam. He only groused because he cared.

"I'm sorry, Dad. Don't worry about it. I can manage." Joann tightened the bow on her apron as if to prove her intention. Driving home her point, she said, "The deal was Nathan would be here to fill in for me."

Dad snorted. "I've been running this store a long time, missy. I think I can handle an afternoon."

"But it's always so busy at the end of August." A child screeched upstairs, punctuating her statement. "I'm not leaving you here with only a delivery boy to help out."

"Well, fine. I'll get Mrs. Delarue to come for the four hours you'll be gone. If she's not available, I'll get Miss Maggie to fill in."

Miss Maggie had been their neighbor for as long as Joann remembered, and always willing to lend a hand. If Joann objected, Dad would only call on another friend, probably one of his buddies who'd do nothing but track in mud and drink coffee. Why did he have to be so friendly?

She rubbed her temples.

Dad's eyes gleamed. He knew he'd won. And here she'd been feeling sorry for him.

"Fine."

As if to contradict Joann's concern about Dad needing Nathan to stay and work, the place completely emptied of customers ten minutes before she needed to go get ready.

An entire swoop of invisible birds flew and dove around in her belly. She had no clue what one wore to a music studio or to meet a businesswoman.

The knot of her apron tie wouldn't loosen. If she couldn't get the thing loose by the time she got to the back, she'd cut it with scissors.

"Nathan," Dad called. "Give Charles the fan belt I set in your front seat."

The rumble of Nathan's reply lost distinction as it traveled to the back hall, but Joann heard him say "late" and "not sure." It set her heart palpitating.

Joann spun on her heel and marched back to the front. "What are you talking about?"

Nathan rubbed the back of his neck. "I said I wasn't sure we'd see Charles."

"Of course we'll see Charles. He and Jerry are meeting us at the record studio."

Another headache plagued Barb and Joann had urged her to stay home.

Nathan put his hands up. "Maybe you should call your sister, just to get the plans straight."

It wasn't necessary to double check. She'd talked to Barb only this morning, but the idea stuck tight as a burr. If Charles had bailed, she'd be on her own.

"Barb would've called me if there were a problem." She resisted picking up the black store phone receiver to check for a dial tone. Irritation bled from her, she knew, but Nathan deserved it. Couldn't he see how nervous she was?

Brow creased, Nathan studied her face, then stared at the floor. He hiked his shoulders. "How about if afterward I treat everyone to dinner?" He wrinkled up his nose like he'd smelled a skunk. "Nothing fancy, though."

The mental picture of Nathan in his canvas pants and work boots dining at a fancy restaurant made her grin. The man was too cute for his own good.

"We'll see," she said. "I'll meet you at the truck in fifteen minutes."

As soon as she got to the house she called Barb, confirming Charles and his roommate would meet Joann at the studio.

***

Halfway through the forty-minute trip to Shreveport, sweat had soaked through Joann's white Sunday gloves and she peeled them off. They were too fancy for the plain yellow dress she wore anyway.

Nathan adjusted the radio dial. "You look like you could conquer the world."

"Thanks." Joann fingered the yellow silk scarf covering her hair.

"I'm proud of you for learning everything you can to make a go of it." He stroked the back of her neck. "You have a smart head on your shoulders."

"Do you really think so? Dad doesn't think I can run the business." Like a bottle uncorked, her feelings tumbled out. "The world doesn't think a woman can run a business, never mind it's fine for her to be the hand that rocks the cradle."

Why on earth had she mentioned a cradle? The last thing she needed was a conversation about babies. One stress-filled topic at a time was plenty.

She'd only meant to make her point about the unfairness of the business world.

Her nerves felt like tiny jolts of electricity trying to poke through her skin, and she was ready for a fight, if need be.

Nathan didn't utter a sound. As calm as could be, he never left off rubbing her tight neck.

Her hands shook. She needed to get ahold of herself. She closed her eyes and inhaled.

Nathan broke the silence. "If there's one thing I know, it's that you can do anything you set your mind to, including running a business."

His words helped calm her from jumping-out-of-her-skin panic to a reasonable level of anxiety. "You're sweet. I appreciate you saying so."

Maybe this meeting would help her secure her place, and the future, of Kincaid's.

He let his hand trail down her arm and she caught it, lacing her fingers in his.

He was a blessing.

Her mouth pursed up in a wry realization. Maybe Dad had been right about sending Nathan along, but she'd die before admitting any such thing.

Along the interstate, the scenery of close-packed pine trees began to thin out, giving way to buildings. Traffic picked up. She'd been to Shreveport plenty of times, but her current purpose gave her fresh eyes. More than a different parish, Joann was entering a different universe. Patty Hightower had managed to make a success of herself while competing in a man's world.

Joann wanted to know how she did it.

CHAPTER SEVENTEEN

The glass entrance door of the small brick building opened straight into a cramped foyer area. Two persimmon-colored couches and an end table bearing an overfull glass ashtray took up most of the space. Framed records and photographs covered the walls. It all left Joann claustrophobic.

"Have a seat." Jerry gestured to the couches. "We're early." He flopped down and pulled out his cigarettes.

Charles shook his head and the guy put his smokes away. Joann wavered, unsure where to sit or *if* she should sit.

Nathan leaned close. "Did you want me to wait outside?"

"Don't be silly."

He touched her elbow and guided her to the empty couch, where they both sat. Charles remained standing and studied a photograph of a white man in a cowboy hat holding a guitar, then moved on to a black gospel trio of women. Another photo captured a girl with the same hairdo as Barb's.

Joann resisted the urge to check her watch. A line of sweat coated her upper lip despite the cool interior of the studio, and she dabbed the moisture with her handkerchief. She patted her hair and smoothed her dress over her thighs.

Her palms were so sweaty.

Almost to herself, she murmured, "I wish Barb could've come." Then, feeling she needed to provide an explanation, she told Jerry, "She loves all kinds of music."

From the belly of the studio, a burst of conversation leaked into the waiting area, followed by singing. A group of four musicians appeared. To Joann's surprise, they weren't dressed up the way she'd expected a musical group to be, but had on jeans and regular shirts. One of the guys wore white penny loafers, and he saw her looking. He grinned. Instead of walking behind his three friends, he made his exit by exhibiting dance moves and fancy footwork. At the door, he paused and bowed his head, tipping an imaginary hat. She averted her gaze, fixating on her lap.

She felt like a country bumpkin.

A slight, brown-haired woman in a blue dress glided into the waiting area. Joann thought she must be an assistant or a secretary. The woman, so sedate and pleasant, provoked an automatic smile from Joann.

Jerry hopped up. "Miss Hightower, this is Joann."

With a wide smile that gave the woman a suddenly impish air, she stuck out a hand. "Call me Patty."

Joann rose to her feet and shook Patty's hand.

Patty said, "So nice to meet you. Come on back."

Attempting to mirror the woman's confidence, Joann straightened her spine and followed. She was rather proud of herself for not glancing back at Nathan for support. Trailing Patty into the recording room, she listened as Patty explained how the studio worked.

The lady was talking about the insulation when she paused. "Sorry. I get carried away."

Patty's laugh reminded Joann of wind chimes.

She waved Joann forward. "Let's go into my office and I'll try to answer your questions."

Joann stammered, "Thank you." The whole experience was so overwhelming, her eyes were probably as big as the LPs hanging out in the foyer.

In the cramped office, reels of tape and papers filled a white painted bookcase. A tiny desk held a phone, untidy stacks of mail, and a half-eaten sandwich, not fresh, going by the dried and curling bread, which somehow brought Joann back to her footing.

Patty gestured to a wooden chair. "Would you like a Coke?"

"That would be lovely."

"Sit tight. Be right back."

While Patty got the drinks, Joann caught herself picking her cuticles, and she tucked her hands under her thighs. She could do this.

Take a breath.

She studied a framed newspaper article showing a photo of Patty and a tall, guitar-holding cowboy at the Louisiana Hayride.

Patty reentered, carrying two ice-cold bottles dripping with condensation. "Here we go." She plunked the drinks onto her desk, slid open the drawer to fish out a bottle opener, and popped off the caps. As she handed a bottle to Joann she announced, "I've got to take these shoes off."

Startled, Joann watched Patty toe off her low dark-brown heels, pick up the other Coke, and settle behind the desk. Patty closed her eyes and drank half the coke before she came up for air.

She released a long sigh. "That's good."

Hiding a smile, Joann sipped her own drink. She liked this lady. She put her at ease. Not enough to take off her own shoes, but enough to banish her nerves.

Patty said, "Tell me, what is it you want to talk about?"

Joann unfolded the list she'd brought along, but all her questions seemed frivolous and silly. She refolded the paper. "I don't really know. I want to be a success, and my sister had the idea of selling records in our general store."

"Your sister?"

Joann nodded. "See, we'd always talked about continuing the family tradition of running the store, and she loves music." Joann shrugged. "She wanted to offer records and record players, but sales haven't been great."

Understatement.

"Is she at the store today?"

"Oh, no." Joann shifted in her seat. Crossed and uncrossed her legs. "She got married."

Patty cocked her head to the side, waiting for more.

"Her husband's in the Air Force. Charles, Jerry's friend? She doesn't work at the store anymore. It's impossible for her to, really, being a military wife. She's having a baby." Joann clamped her mouth closed to stop her rambling. Patty didn't need to hear about the entire family situation.

"I see." Patty frowned at her Coke and took another swig.

"I need to show my dad I can run the store. Honestly, I've been running the store for years, but he doesn't see it. Selling records was meant to prove I could do it."

"But sales are bad."

"Sales are bad."

"And it was your sister's idea, but she's not working at the store anymore?"

Joann stiffened. "Selling records isn't a bad idea."

"Not at all." Patty's kept her bland demeanor and an agreeable tone. "Never can have too much music."

Joann relaxed a notch.

"But if it's your sister's idea, and she's not part of the business anymore, would you still want to go in that direction?"

Joann's mouth dropped open. "I don't know. I hadn't really thought about it."

"I'll be honest here. It's a hard row to hoe, being in business as a woman. I can tell you're committed to the family business, but it helps to understand what customers want. Add in what you're passionate about, what you believe in and you might have a chance." Patty rolled her Coke bottle between her hands. "If you're trying to prove something to your dad, things can get sticky. I couldn't give an opinion there. But if you want to own part of the business or have a say, you'll have to convince him." She wrinkled her nose. "We can put in all the work, but it doesn't mean we'll get a fair shake."

Joann knew that. No woman could get a bank account, much less business loans, without a male relative backing her. And some businessmen didn't like working with women business owners.

Patty sat up. "If you want to make sales, find a product or service people need and fill the gap. But you already knew that, I'd bet."

"Yes." Joann did, but had been so excited about Barb's idea she hadn't checked into the logistics of the project. If she told herself the whole truth, she'd probably said yes to Barb—at least in part—to try to close the growing distance she'd sensed between them. And as it turned out, running the store together had been more Joann's dream than Barb's.

After Joann and Patty talked for a while, Patty took Nathan and Joann on a tour while Charles and Jerry went outside to grab a cigarette.

The live room, where musicians performed, contained a variety of stands and microphones, but had plenty of space. On the other hand, the control room packed a huge amount of technology into the square footage. Joann loitered near the doorway, afraid to enter lest she bump against a switch or button. Nathan showed no such reticence. As he listened intently to Patty and examined the control board, Joann returned to the live room, content to watch them through the large plate-glass window between the rooms.

"Hey." Jerry stuck his head in. "Where's Nathan?"

Joann gestured to the window. "In there with Patty. They'll be out in a minute."

He came over and stood by her. Charles entered and joined them, trailing cigarette smoke. Expression grim, Charles took another puff before stubbing his cigarette in a metal ashtray and beckoning to Nathan through the glass.

Jerry fidgeted, his legs like a jerky puppet on stage. As soon as Nathan and Patty came out, he blurted, "On the radio they said the president made it so men getting married after today won't be exempt from the draft anymore. Things are heating up." The wrinkles in Jerry's forehead piled up. He shook his head at Joann. "You shoulda married him last week."

Inhaling sharply, Joann put a hand to her throat. "What are you talking about?"

She turned to Charles. He opened his mouth, but Jerry broke in before he could speak.

"The president. He's running out of men to fight in Vietnam. From now on, they'll even take the married men. A wedding ring won't matter." Jerry feigned a punch to Nathan's arm. "Better go ahead and enlist in the Air Force, man. Better chances to make it to the end."

Joann grasped the crook of Nathan's elbow and held tight.

What did it mean?

She cast a questioning glance at Nathan, but he only clasped her hand, rubbing her knuckles. The motion chafed, but she didn't tell him to stop.

She wouldn't let him go for anything.

In the parking lot, Joann forced a smile and thanked Jerry and Charles for coming, all plans to visit a restaurant forgotten.

Like playing a part in a stage production, she babbled with inappropriate cheer, "Charles, you take care of my sister now. Tell her I'll come to see her as soon as I can."

Charles kneaded his hat in his fists and nodded. "I will."

"See you later." Jerry gave Nathan a light punch on the shoulder and winked at Joann, seemingly unaware of the turmoil he'd set loose.

On the drive home, Joann scooted close to Nathan, but he held himself so stiff he could've been carved of wood. Every so often, the truck drifted and he jerked it into alignment with the road. When she slid away from him, he snaked out his arm and caught her, drawing her close. Mindless of the heat and their sweaty skin, she laid her head on his shoulder and kept it there all the way back home, her mind and emotions numb save for the instinct to keep him close.

Nathan pulled around to the back of the store and cut the engine. They sat in somber silence.

Joann said, "If we'd gotten married, you'd be safe now. I would've done it to keep you safe."

And she would have. She'd walk through fire to keep him safe.

Motionless, Nathan remained silent, every line of his body a "keep out" sign.

She swallowed hard and whispered, "Is that why you were talking about marriage?"

Nathan shifted around to face her. Reaching out one finger, he traced her jaw with infinite gentleness, and turned her face toward him. He searched her eyes, his face a picture of anguish. The feelings were true, and raw, and real, but she couldn't tell what he was thinking.

She lowered her lashes, trying not to cry, but tears streaked her cheeks all the same.

"Jo, look at me."

She did.

"I wouldn't want you to marry me to save me. I want you to marry me because you want to be my wife." Featherlight, he brushed her tears away. "I never want to rush you."

"What are you going to do? Will you do like Jerry says and join the Air Force?"

"I don't know. I need to think about it." The muscles in his jaw flexed. "But if I'm called, I'll do my duty."

CHAPTER EIGHTEEN

At the store, and everywhere, whenever Joann and Nathan were together, they'd returned to earlier days, it seemed, stealing kisses like high school kids, talking hardly at all, relying on touches and glances instead of words. At times she felt reckless, on the edge of something beautiful and terrible.

One morning she approached the store, intent on grabbing another moment with him, her weak knees the result of anticipation or anxiety, she didn't know.

It had been two weeks since they'd gone to Shreveport, and Nathan hadn't enlisted in the USAF as Jerry suggested.

Joann couldn't imagine how Mr. Poole would react if Nathan volunteered. The war, his war, had ruined their family and destroyed the man.

She suppressed a shudder.

Nathan caught her in the back room. It was impossible for her to pull away.

When they came up for air, breathless and bothered, she said, "We'd better get to work."

"Sure, boss." Nathan grinned.

He went about his work acting like nothing was wrong at all. Like they had all the time in the world.

Later, during a slow spell, Joann sat at the checkers table, leafing through Barb's cookbook.

Nathan set down a crate of sodas next to the cooler and leaned over her. "What are you doing?"

"Searching for a recipe."

"I like cherry pie."

She swatted his chest, letting her hand rest there, right over his heart, fancying she could count the beats. "It's for Gospel Reunion Days."

It was only September, and the event wasn't until the second weekend of October, but Joann wanted to add a few notes in the cookbook as well. Besides, no time like the present.

People from nearby parishes came in droves to Pecan Ridge for the yearly event. She needed a crowd-pleaser. The barnlike community center sat off the interstate, back from the road, right in the center of a hayfield. For weeks afterward, the surrounding field would remain flattened by the foot traffic and cars. Everyone came. All the women brought their best recipes to the table.

So would she.

Nathan cocked his head, pretending to read the book. "I bet you can't make a cherry pie."

Joann snorted. "Of course I can."

"Prove it."

"Go put those drinks in the cooler."

Whistling the tune from *The Andy Griffith Show*, he sauntered over to the case and did as she said.

Joann shook her head and went back to the cookbook, coming across an inscription.

Remember, you'll shed fewer tears if you cut the root end of the onion last.

Was it a literal fact or a saying? Next time she peeled an onion she'd try it to see.

Onions made her think of crying, and crying made her think of a gospel song Elvis had recently remade. She picked up a pen and scribbled in the margin.

Not all crying in church is bad.

"Crying in the Chapel" 1965

They could all use tears of joy. Reminders of the old songs and the messages they carried could only be a good thing.

She checked her Timex.

Barb was across the street at the house, left there with strict directions to put her feet up for twenty minutes. Time was almost up.

Jerry, the friendly roommate who had been driving Barb mad, had finally found new digs and moved out. To ease things further, Charles often brought her around to spend the day with Joann. Barb did light work in the store as Joann and Nathan both kept close watch, insisting she rest often and not tax herself.

Joann closed the cookbook and hid it in a cubbyhole underneath the register. She didn't want her sister to see it.

Once Nathan had gone home, Barb clutched a bag of Epsom salt as she squeezed past an endcap display of cold remedies. The blue striped tent dress she wore announced rather than concealed her pregnancy. She'd regained a little of the weight she'd lost, Joann was happy to see.

Joann took the Epsom salt from her. "Tell me what else you need, and I'll get it for you."

Barb's lower lip jutted out. "I'm perfectly capable of carrying a bag of Epsom salt."

A sharp retort parked on the tip of Joann's tongue. She held it there. The longer the day, the crankier Barb got. Annoying, but understandable.

She changed the subject. "Are you and Charles coming to the Gospel Reunion Days next month?"

Tucking limp, uncurled hair behind her ear, Barb said, "I hope so."

"Remember when we'd sit in the window seat and listen to the late-night players?"

Barb smiled. "There were always stragglers, but Daddy made us come home. We could still hear them."

"Lullabies."

Barb cradled her belly, a faraway wistfulness in her eyes. The expression tugged at Joann's heartstrings. She feared more than normal pregnancy changes haunted her sister. Barb hadn't suffered fits of melancholy before.

Joann said, "Well, you must come. I'm going to bake some pies. Tell Charles I'll make a coconut cake."

With a soft side hug, Barb rested her head on Joann's shoulder. "You're so good to me."

This, more than all the mopiness and morning sickness, struck fear into Joann.

She had to talk to Charles when he came to pick up Barb.

Joann kept her arm firmly around Barb as if she might fly off if she let go. "It'll be cold cuts and ice cream for supper. You're staying. No arguing. I'll make lemonade, unless you're sick of it."

Mrs. Delarue had recommended cold lemonade and ginger snaps for morning sickness, and Barb had taken the advice to heart.

"Lemonade sounds fine."

After Charles came and the store closed up snug for the night, Joann kept the mood as jolly as she could through the evening meal.

With *Perry Mason* coming on the set, Joann suggested they have ice cream in the living room. After a while, Charles excused himself to step outside, and she wordlessly got up, gathering the empty bowls and spoons.

She murmured, "Be right back."

Kitchen duty would provide a handy excuse if she needed one, but she shouldn't have bothered. Barb and Dad remained absorbed in the television drama.

She went through the kitchen and out the back door, taking her bowl of melted ice cream. Cats were always hanging about. Stepping around the side of the house, she called the cats, loud enough for Charles to hear her.

The creak of the swing and a drift of cigarette smoke gave him away.

"Hey, Charles." Joann set the bowl down on the front step. "I'm glad to catch a minute with you."

"Yeah?" Charles stubbed out his half-smoked cigarette. "What's up?"

Now she'd cornered him, she began to second guess if she should put her oar in, but the image of Barb's unhappy face and uncared-for hair drove her to speak. "Is there anything I can do to help you and Barb? She seems...down."

Charles inhaled and released a long, deflating breath. A wry smile tugged at his lips. "I'd meant to ask you but hadn't figured on how to bring it up. I don't know how you have such great timing. You always seem to know when Barb needs something."

Because she's my sister.

Joann rested her hip on the porch column closest to the swing. "Go ahead and ask me, then."

Charles fiddled with his cigarettes, tamping the pack. He took one out, then put it back. "She wants to do Lamaze, and the lady in the class says it's better to have a friend or sister with her."

"What classes? What's Lamaze?"

He got out a cigarette and lit it. "Something she heard about from the other wives." The end of his cigarette crackled as he took a deep drag. "Natural childbirth."

Joann remembered hearing about it. A sort of support for the woman in labor while she was in the hospital.

Even with Charles turned away from the porch light, Joann could see he'd blanched ghost white. She clamped her jaw shut to keep from laughing.

"Of course I'll go with her." It bothered Joann that Barb hadn't said anything her, and worry pushed up into her chest. "But I think something else must be wrong."

Charles's eyes widened. "What?"

Joann cleared her throat. "A lot has happened. It's been a big change for Barb, marriage, baby, running a house."

"I know. I try to encourage her."

"She told me you've been encouraging her, but she's pressuring herself to keep house. She can do accounts like nobody's business and remembers when we need to reorder supplies better than I ever could, but never did learn to cook. No time."

"Her cooking is fine! I don't complain."

"Maybe not, but she wants to make everything perfect for you. She wants to make you happy." She left off the part about Barb feeling she'd never measure up to his mother.

Charles fiddled with his cigarettes before shoving them into his pocket. "What do you think I should do?"

Joann couldn't tell him to stop bragging on his mom's cooking.

The concern Barb had inherited a tendency toward sad spells from their father poked its ugly head into her mind, but that couldn't be it. And she wouldn't appreciate Joann mentioning such a thing. Crabby and sassy maybe, but melancholy had never been one of Barb's many moods. Joann frowned at the haze blanketing the stars. Her sister would snap out of it.

Joann said, "Let her be herself. Tell her it's all right to enjoy the same things she did before she got married." She forced a grin. "And if you want to keep from getting a stomach ache, don't let her try cooking anything fancy."

Charles chuckled. "It's not so bad."

Joann put her hands up in surrender. "It's your stomach."

***

On Barb's next appointment to the doctor, Joann accompanied her to the base. The girls walked into the big brick building and entered a warren of halls full of men in uniform and people in civilian clothes.

Barb hooked elbows with Joann. "I'm so glad you came with me." Her complexion had a dewy glow.

Joann gave her sister a gentle bump. "Anytime. I'm always here for you. Count on it."

Attending a birth had never been high on Joann's to-do list, but Barb wanted her there. She wouldn't miss it for all the sweet tea in the world.

"I feel better already, knowing you'll be at the birth." Her brow wrinkled. "Charles is supposed to meet us at the doctor's. I hope he can get away. He's supposed to have a lunch break at eleven thirty."

They entered a waiting area with three rows of green and orange chairs lined up and facing a reception counter. Joann stayed to the side as Barb spoke with the receptionist.

The patient waiting area was empty, except for a young woman near her time. She attempted to corral her two young children, a boy and a girl, but they wouldn't have it. Like floppy rag dolls, they squirmed and fussed.

The mother tossed an apologetic smile at Joann and Barb and said, "We've been here a while. They're hungry."

The older one, the boy, rubbed his red eyes.

Not a clock in sight, but it was near noon. Joann smiled at her and perched on a chair, glad Barb was only here to talk with the doctor about Joann being her birthing coach. The appointment shouldn't take long. The place had a deserted air.

Charles strode in, and Joann did a double take at his appearance. He seemed taller and older somehow, until his eyes lit on Barb and his entire demeanor shifted, softening. The breath caught in Joann's throat.

The little girl began crying in earnest. The mother scolded the boy for pulling his sister's hair and he joined the cryfest.

It was like being compressed in a before and after comparison.

Barb greeted Charles with a kiss on the cheek and motioned for Joann to join them, so she did.

A no-nonsense nurse led them into an office. "Have a seat. The doctor will come in to speak with you in a moment." The door clicked shut behind her.

Not very friendly, but Joann kept her observation to herself.

The place seemed to set Barb on edge, even with Charles holding her hand, and Joann had to school herself not to squirm in the rigid plastic chair.

Minutes passed before the white-coated doctor entered. He had the physique of a retired football player, not at all what Joann expected. He said, "It's nice to see you, Charles. What can I do for you today?"

Barb leaned forward. "Dr. Willard, this is my sister, Joann."

The doctor raised bristly eyebrows, sparing Joann a whisper of a glance. "Oh?"

"Yes. She's going to Lamaze classes with me. She's my coach."

The stone-faced doctor cut his eyes at Charles. "There's no need for a coach. I've been delivering babies for quite some time. Visitors aren't allowed in delivery, you know."

Joann's mouth opened to object, but Charles beat her to the punch. "She wouldn't be a visitor. She's my wife's coach, and they will both continue to attend the classes until Barb delivers. I'd like for Joann to be with Barb during her labor for as long as possible."

The men assessed each other with cool, silent communication. The doctor outranked Charles, to be sure, but Charles didn't flinch.

He was a good man, one who would stand up for Barb, and the knowledge set Joann's confidence firmly in him.

Nothing would happen to Barb on his watch. Not if he could help it. She wanted to cheer, but kept her face straight.

The doctor sighed. "We can arrange something." He pinned Barb with a stern look. "Make sure you go to every class. No skipping. And keep all your appointments."

An unusually meek Barb bobbed her head.

The doctor stood, extending his hand toward Charles. Charles followed suit, and the men shook hands.

The whole scenario was such a change from interactions with their long-time family doctor, a portly fellow who brought a sense of peace into the room with him, a person you could trust to help you. This man was an entirely different sort. If she were free to speak her mind, her comment would leave a scorch trail, which wouldn't help her sister's situation.

Luckily for Barb and Joann, the Lamaze classes would be held at the instructor's home.

CHAPTER NINETEEN

The classes were mostly breathing and focusing. Some massage techniques. Joann wasn't sure distracting Barb from pain would work. When they were kids, Barb had fallen out of a tree and broken her arm. From the way she carried on at that incident—and every bump and bruise since—Joann didn't see how foregoing medication was possible. But then, medications during pregnancy were scary as all get out, so Joann understood. Thalidomide babies proved how dangerous drugs could be. The wrong pill at the wrong time could cause devastating birth defects.

At least Barb's morning sickness had finally abated, right in time to plan attending the Gospel Reunion. She'd enjoy the event. She wasn't home today, but tomorrow, for the first time since she'd gotten married, Barb was staying for the night. Charles had drawn an overnight assignment and hadn't wanted her at the apartment alone.

Smiling to herself, Joann poured cranberries into a metal colander and rinsed them in the sink. At first, she'd thought to use canned cherries, but when she'd found a recipe for mock cherry pie in *Mrs. Canfield's Cookery Book*, she'd decided on using the old recipe instead. She'd show Nathan.

Can't make a cherry pie. Hmph.

Not only could she make a cherry pie, she didn't even need cherries to do so. She grinned at the idea. When she told Nathan so after he'd eaten the pie, he'd get a kick out of her cherry-less experiment.

The next day, a few minutes before two o'clock, Joann flipped the closed sign on the door of the store. On the bottom of a flyer for the Gospel Reunion, she added a note saying the store was closed for the event and taped it above the regular sign.

She stepped into the office and found Dad at the desk, poring over a stack of checks.

She said, "Meet me at home? Barb should be there soon."

He nodded, giving a distracted wave.

"Don't take too long, Dad. I can finish up the books tomorrow for you if you like."

"I'm about done."

"All right."

Joann felt like skipping across the street to their white, two-story home. Soon, Barb would be under the same roof with her. She was coming home.

She did a little jig. It was like being a teenager again, both of them together.

For supper, she emptied a can of stew into a pot and set it to simmer, then dashed upstairs for a quick bath and change of clothes.

When she came back downstairs, she caught Dad, his tongue peeking from the corner of his mouth, examining the pie and the two other Tupperware containers of sweets on the countertop.

"Don't you dare!"

With a sheepish look, he backed away from the food. "Was only looking."

She plucked an overripe banana from the fruit bowl on the kitchen table and handed it to him. "Go watch TV. I'll bring your supper in a minute."

Barb wandered into the kitchen. She must've been in the powder room.

Joann said, "Hey, sis. When did you get here?"

"A minute ago."

No greeting hug, but that was typical. She'd been more herself of late, and happier. Her cheeks had even plumped out.

Barb surveyed the Tupperware. "How many desserts did you make?"

"The cookies and chocolate cake are for the event." Joann opened the cabinet and got bowls out.

If she didn't spoon up the soup, her family would start drooling on the goodies.

She passed Barb a full bowl. "Here. This one's for Dad. Get some crackers from the canister."

Barb tipped her chin down and eyed Joann suspiciously. "Who's the pie for?"

Joann stuck her nose in the air. "If you must know, Nathan." She opened a drawer and found a marker and a notepad. She scribbled a note saying *For Nathan, a pie as requested* and placed it on the box. "And I made it from scratch." She found cellophane tape in the junk drawer and taped the note to the box.

Barb put the bowl of soup down and popped open the container of cookies, selecting one. "Better watch it. You'll get domesticated."

"Not likely." Joann snorted. "Nathan bet me I couldn't do it. I'm proving him wrong."

Barb choked out a laugh, spewing cookie crumbs. "I should've known."

Joann flicked a dishtowel at her.

It was wonderful to have the old Barb back.

"Go give Dad his soup."

The girls took Barb's car to the community center. It was odd to think of Charles's red coupe as Barb's car, but she maneuvered the vehicle as if it were as easy as popping on a new hat.

Dad would come later in his sedan where he could stretch out and enjoy a respite from their chatter, or so he said. Joann knew it was because he understood how the sisters missed each other.

A few trucks were in the parking area, Nathan's among them. The girls entered the large building through the propped open door, Barb carrying the Tupperware of cookies and Joann the cake. Joann would make another trip for the pie.

The event wasn't for another hour, but rows of chairs waited in formation for attendees and an uneven line of tables snaked its way along one wall. Within the next thirty minutes, the tables would be groaning under the weight of homemade goodies brought by the women of the community. No prizes were given, but a secret tally would provide gossip fodder and bragging rights until the next event.

The girls placed the Tupperware of cookies and the chocolate cake on a table.

A friend from high school, a baby on her hip, waved and started toward them.

Joann nodded at her and said to Barb, "You catch up while I fetch Nathan's pie."

More cars had arrived, and on her way to retrieve the pie, Joann chatted for a moment or two with people. She'd almost made it back into the community center when Cora Lee stopped her.

"I see Barb came." The corners of her painted lips curled up in a catty smile. She arched an eyebrow. "She's blooming, isn't she?"

Joann set her face in a smile so brittle it might crack. "Sorry. Can't talk, Cora Lee." She lifted the box and the note came loose, fluttering to the ground.

Cora Lee bent over and snatched it up. "You lost this."

Too late, Joann reached for the note.

Cora Lee was already scanning it. "For Nathan. Well, isn't that sweet?" She simpered.

Do not engage.

Joann used her best customer service voice. "May I have my paper, please, Cora Lee?"

Not put off at all, Cora Lee laid the note on the box and pressed the tape with a finger to restick it. "There you go."

The sooner Joann could get this pie to Nathan, the better.

Inside the community hall, she scanned the clusters of people and spied him leaning against the wall with a couple of other guys, talking.

She hesitated. If she approached, surely the guys would tease. But why did she care? With a toss of her head, she strode straight over.

Extending the box toward Nathan, she said, "For you."

She'd gotten too close, the box practically touching his plaid shirt, and he drew back his elbows in order to grab the pie.

"Thanks. I can't wait. Come on. Let's find a seat." He lifted the lid and smacked his lips.

"You could take it home."

"Nothing doing. Where's a fork?"

Joann found utensils on a table and brought a fork back to Nathan. By then, a small crowd of onlookers had gathered.

He dug in and shoved a huge bite into his mouth. His eyes rounded and his eyebrows shot up. After a beat, he nodded and swallowed.

Joann crossed her arms. "See?"

"Yep." Nathan scooped up another big bite and put it in his mouth.

Barb joined the spectators. A guy peered into the box. Nathan hunched over it as if to keep it to himself and lighthearted laughter erupted among the group.

After he'd gobbled down about two servings of the pie, Nathan waved his fork in the direction of the tables. "I think this deserves coffee." He closed the box and took it with him.

Barb winked at Joann and hurried after Nathan. Waiting until he had both hands occupied, Barb opened the box and snuck a bite. Joann shook her head at them both. The way those two carried on, no one could tell they weren't siblings.

Next thing, Barb rushed to a trashcan and bent over.

Joann rushed to her. They'd done too much today, and now Barb was sick again. Why had Joann insisted they come?

She rubbed her sister's back. "Are you okay?"

Instead of Barb being upset, as Joann expected, she came up laughing. "Oh, Jo! What did you do to the pie?"

"What do you mean?"

"It's terrible!"

"What?"

"The pie. It's not right." Barb wiped at her mouth with her arm.

Burning with embarrassment from her hive-splotched chest to the roots of her ginger hair, Joann marched over to Nathan, and they had a tug of war with the box.

"Let go," she growled.

Reluctantly, he gave in. She flipped the lid up and whipped her hand out in Nathan's direction, palm up, like a surgeon waiting for a scalpel. Fork ready, she cut a fragment of pie and deposited the morsel on her tongue. Tartness shrank her taste buds and moisture deserted her mouth.

She scrambled for a napkin. As discreetly as possible in a room of spectators, she spit out the bite. Not enough sugar. Maybe she'd forgotten to put any in.

Mindful of the growing audience, she turned on Nathan, hissing, "Why didn't you say it was so tart?"

How on earth had he managed to choke down the awful stuff?

He shrugged and squirmed like a child being scolded.

Joann picked up the pie, box and all, and tossed it into the trash.

An onlooker spoke up. "Don't worry, Joann. Happens to the best of us."

Joann froze. Cora Lee.

Voice dripping with glee, Cora Lee continued. "Maybe he doesn't need any sugar, because he's so sweet on you."

A ripple of laugher came from the crowd.

One man gripped Nathan's neck playfully, and another slapped his back. The women gave Joann a wide berth. An invisible circle of humiliation surrounded her until Barb snugged her arm around Joann's waist.

"Don't feel bad, Jo. It was an honest mistake."

"I didn't need to let my pride trip me in front of the entire tri-parish community, though."

"Just remember, no matter what, you'll probably always be a better cook than me."

At that, both girls burst into laughter.

A man onstage did a microphone check. All in a flurry, spectators found seats and performers gathered instruments or headed backstage.

Nathan's crew left him standing alone. He smiled at Joann.

With a final side squeeze Barb said, "I'm going to find a spot close to the middle and save our seats. There's Dad. I'll go see if he wants to sit with us."

"All right. You go on, then." Joann waved her off as Nathan approached.

When he got in reach, she gave him a light punch to the bicep. "After you tasted it, why did you keep eating?"

"I didn't want to hurt your feelings, or cause you embarrassment."

"I managed the embarrassed part all on my own."

He slung a proprietary arm around her shoulders. "Come on, let's go listen to some gospel." He kissed the top of her head. "I don't care if you can bake a pie or not, you're still my favorite girl."

Joann drew back and stuck out her tongue at him. "I can too bake. I'd had a distracting day, is all."

"All right."

He tucked her to his side, and she stayed close, even though it was certain to fan gossip and teasing over the pie incident, a cooking experiment that would haunt her forever.

At the first chord of an old hymn, the music took Joann back and simultaneously grounded her in the present. The only thing better than being in the arms of her family was to be in the arms of Jesus, and the music reminded her how blessed she was.

Nothing was as glorious as being with loved ones, celebrating God's goodness in the company of believers.

At the close of the evening, as she retrieved her empty Tupperware, she overheard a plump woman say, "I wish we could hear these groups every week. Pity we can only enjoy the music once a year."

A spark ignited in Joann's brain. Familiar faces peppered the crowd, people she'd see at the store. What if more of them wanted to extend their enjoyment of the Gospel Reunion?

If offered an opportunity, the performers might want to record their songs, and people might want to support musicians they knew and loved.

The seeds of a market research plan began to grow in her mind.

CHAPTER TWENTY

By the first of October, Joann had contacted the musical performers from Gospel Days, save for one she hadn't been able acquire a phone number for. Fridays were busy, but she'd taken the day, spending the early morning on laundry and mopping the linoleum, a task long overdue. Cleaning helped order her mind. She had a lunch meeting with Patty Hightower, but first she needed to write a letter to the last group on her list. Letter writing was a thing she rather loathed, but if she were to be a businesswoman, she may as well get used to it.

She settled at the writing desk tucked into the corner of her bedroom and labored over paper for half an hour before folding and sealing the letter into an envelope. She'd go by the post office before her meeting.

Humming a happy tune, she tucked the letter into the folder containing her list of prospects.

Patty would have to go for her idea.

***

This time, the drive to Shreveport didn't pluck her nerves. Not much. Parking at the brick luncheonette at the corner of two busy streets did, but she managed.

The place was crowded. She'd hoped for a seat near the window, planning to keep watch for Patty, but the waitress led her to a table in the center. Too nervous to complain or make a request, Joann sat, fumbled with her oversized purse, looped it on the back of the chair, then removed it to put at her feet.

The bored waitress passed her a menu. "What can I get you?"

"A Tab, for now. I'll order later. I'm waiting for someone."

Diners came and went, while Joann nervously picked at the tablecloth. It was one thing to collect data from customers who might or might not want to buy records, and from performers who might or might not want to make a record. It was another thing entirely to attempt a business proposal.

The ice cubes in Joann's glass had melted into the last dregs of her soda by the time Patty hurried through the door and began weaving through the tables toward her.

"Sorry I'm late." She plopped into the chair opposite Joann.

Right on cue, the waitress appeared.

Patty said, "The special's fine."

The waitress asked Joann, "And you?"

"The same." She hoped it wasn't liver and onions.

As soon as the waitress departed, Patty lasered in on Joann, in her forthright, friendly way. "What's your idea?"

It had sounded so logical before, but now? Joann hid her shaking hands in her lap.

"I have a proposal." She picked up her bag and drew out a sheaf of papers. "I remembered what you said about finding a niche, and I've done a little research." She spread the papers on the table. "The ones marked in blue are groups who are interested in making a record." Joann went through the proposal, citing the long history of the gospel reunion, the surveys she'd conducted of their regular customers, and the musical groups she'd contacted. "It seems if I provide records of favorite groups, my customers will buy, especially with Christmas coming up."

"That all sounds wonderful, but what did you want from me?"

"If you offered a discount to the musicians I referred, everyone might benefit. I'd send you business, the musicians would get a discount, and I'd get product to sell."

Patty grinned. "I like your initiative. Usually, I wouldn't go for this kind of thing."

"Oh." Joann wilted.

"But I think anyone with this much spunk and smarts can make this car go. I'll do it."

"Really?"

"Let's try it for say, six months, and see how it goes. That should carry you through Christmas and into the Easter season."

Joann suppressed a wiggle of joy and extended her hand for a shake.

Patty grasped it, grinning, and pumped three times.

If determination and hard work had anything to do with it, this idea would be a success.

Now all Joann could do was wait and see.

And pray.

CHAPTER TWENTY-ONE

All the birth classes in the world didn't prepare Joann for seeing Barb in pain. They'd been at the hospital for hours. At first, Barb had been excited, joking about wanting to get the baby out before Halloween the next day, talking to her tummy and calling the baby "Pumpkin."

Barb wasn't excited now.

In an attempt to soothe, Joann stroked her sister's hair back from her forehead.

Barb swatted her away as if she were a pesky fly. Panting, she gasped out, "Don't touch me."

Joann could do nothing but hold her sister's hand and watch the sweat drip down her neck. Four other women in various stages of labor shared the large room, separated by dividers of thin blue fabric curtains. People came in and out, shoes squeaking on the shiny floor.

Barb cried.

Joann dabbed at her tears with a Kleenex and alternated silent curses toward Charles and all men in general with prayers for mercy.

Barb gasped out, "My head hurts. Did you tell them the lights are too bright?"

"I did, sissy."

The last attendant had only shrugged when Joann had told her about the lights.

Joann picked up the cup on the side table. "Do you want some ice?"

A nurse came in. "Miss Kincaid, would you mind stepping out? I need to check on sister, here." While not exactly oozing warmth, she patted Barb's foot with kindness. "We'll see how progress is coming along."

Joann headed down the hall to the waiting room. The white-tiled floor and bustling nurse's station brought a certain sense of security.

Charles sat in one of the hard plastic chairs and he sprang up like a jack-in-the-box. "How is she?"

"They say all is going well. The nurse is checking her now."

He collapsed back into the chair and put his head in his hands. The man was a pile of misery, and Joann forgave him, a little. She recognized her anger was misplaced fear, but it felt a fine thing to hang onto.

Joann sipped a Tab, but threw it away half-finished and returned to the nurses' station. "May I go back to my sister? She's in the labor room."

The young nurse manning the desk put down a file. "Name?"

Joann told her.

The lady hurried down the hall only to come back and tell her Barb had been moved to delivery.

"Shouldn't be long now," she chirped in a cheery tone. "You can take a seat in the main waiting room." The nurse pointed back the way Joann had come from. "You know where it is?"

Joann nodded. The tension encircling her head eased a fraction. It would be over soon.

She found Charles in the same spot, and in the same condition.

He leapt to his feet when he saw her. "Is she okay?"

Now, with Barb nearing the finish line, the sight of his scruffy face and panicked eyes sparked tenderness in Joann. "Yes. It won't be long now. I'm going to call Dad."

"Here." Charles fumbled in his pockets and produced a handful of change. "When can I see her?"

"They'll let us know." She patted his arm. "I'll be right back."

***

The blanket-wrapped bundle in Barb's arms let out a small cry and she shushed it, already an expert. Joann marveled at how Barb had instinctively transformed into the role of mother as easily as slipping on a new pair of shoes. A beaming Charles stood beside the bed, while Dad sat in a chair nearby, his chest so puffed the buttons of his gray wool cardigan strained at the buttonholes.

Dad said, "Susan is a fine name. A fine name."

From her perch on the end of the bed, Joann craned her neck around, watching the baby girl suck her fist. The purple shadows under Barb's eyes were like bruises. She gazed at Charles in a silent plea. Clearly, she wanted him to send them away, but he either didn't register her wishes or was distracted by the baby.

Joann stood. "Come on, Dad. We'll let Barb rest and come back tomorrow. Visiting hours end soon and it's time to think about supper, isn't it?"

"I guess so." Dad gently tapped the baby's nose. "What do you say, little one?"

A thin cry erupted from the baby's tiny pink mouth and Dad chuckled. "I thought so."

Had he gone gooey over her and Barb in the same way? Affection for her father swept over her. He'd been a good dad, working long days, yet finding energy for bedtime reads of *The Gingerbread Man* a thousand times.

Joann kissed Barb's cheek. "Call if you need me."

After a week in the hospital, Barb insisted on going home, even though she could've remained another day or two. Just as stubborn, Joann insisted on staying with her at the apartment to help with the baby, and Barb gave in without a fight.

Two weeks into Joann's visit, the sisters began rubbing each other the wrong way.

Barb stirred a spoonful of sugar into her coffee. "I'm perfectly fine. You need to go help Dad with the store." She took a sip, grimaced, and set the cup down. "I don't know why I put sugar in this."

The small dining alcove in the kitchen barely had room for a two-person table. A table presently crowded with baby bottles, a pile of men's socks, and cards of congratulations. Joann began sorting the socks.

Barb said, "There aren't any matches. Those need darning."

Withdrawing her hands from the pile, Joann asked, "Where's your sewing kit?"

"I'm not letting you darn my husband's socks."

Her own coffee gone cold, Joann got up from the table. "All right."

She knew better than to ask Barb what needed to be done. It would only elicit a sharp retort from Barb, insisting she didn't need anything.

Joann got busy stripping beds and remaking them with spare sheets from home. She was bundling dirty sheets up for the laundromat when the baby's cries pierced the air. Feeding time.

While Barb tended to Susan, Joann took the opportunity to sweep and mop. What would Barb do about it? Dirty the clean floors in rebellion? The entire apartment was so compact doing the floors didn't take long. Other than to retrieve the coffee cups and a dirty plate, she didn't dare touch the clutter on the table.

After rinsing the dishes and setting them in the drainer, Joann approached Barb's room and eased the door open.

Tenderness and peace emanated from Barb as she rocked a milk-sated Susan. Never taking her eyes from the baby, she motioned for Joann to come in.

Reluctant to break the spell, Joann hesitated on the threshold, but she did as Barb wished. Together, the sisters watched the sleeping baby, and Joann wondered what was wrong with her that she didn't feel the maternal tug so many others obviously did, and expected her to as well. She loved the tiny person, and would never shirk her responsibility, but all the predictions about catching baby fever hadn't borne fruit.

It would come, she told herself.

She opened her arms. "Can I hold her?"

Barb smiled and let her take the baby. They traded places, Joann snuggling the child close, breathing in the sweet scent of baby as she relaxed into the chair.

"I'll grab a shower." Barb opened the closet and selected a navy knit shirt and a long skirt of the same color.

At least it wasn't another nightgown. Some days Barb never dressed, which was understandable. Joann rocked the baby. Who could worry about clothes when a baby needed tending?

When Barb returned, she'd pulled her hair back and put on lipstick. Joann had a premonition her nights on the lumpy couch in Barb's living room were numbered.

Barb took the sleeping baby and laid her in the bedside bassinette. She gestured for Joann to follow her out of the room.

In the kitchen, Barb turned on the oven and removed a casserole from the Frigidaire, setting it on the stovetop. She peeled back the foil and peeked in before covering it again.

As if there hadn't been a peaceful interlude, Barb picked up the earlier argument. "You have to go look after

Dad. You know how he gets when the store is busy. He won't eat right. Nobody's bringing *him* casseroles."

"I know."

"I'm heating this up and you can take a plate home for him. I don't want you to worry about me."

"I like staying here with you."

Barb treated Joann to an eye roll worthy of younger years. "Too bad. Go home. The week before Thanksgiving everybody and their cousin is in the store. Dad needs your help."

Immediately, Joann came back with, "Nathan's there."

It shocked her, the way he'd come to mind. The way she depended on him.

Barb retrieved a small Tupperware container from the cabinet. "If it makes you feel better, you can come back later in the week." She put the container down and took both of Joann's hands in hers. "I promise to call if I need you, but I'll be happier knowing you're taking care of Dad and the store. After all, I have Charles here." She squeezed Joann's hands and let go, turning to put the casserole in the oven.

Charles's heart was in the right place, but he had work. No longer than three days before, he'd received a phone call and had to report to duty immediately. Barb had a blind spot and, unbalanced by the realization she'd expected Nathan to fill in for her, Joann wondered if she did as well.

It wasn't wise to depend too much on Nathan. He hadn't brought up their relationship again, and Joann wasn't about to push. Without Barb at home, she couldn't bear to lose Nathan as well. It would be best to remember he was a friend, a dear one, and a temporary employee.

An employee who stole kisses in the storeroom. A flame of wanting heated her core, and she blew out a breath through pursed lips, as if it would cool her off. It did nothing to ease the ache in her heart. Wanting led to nothing but more wanting, and she reminded herself to be content. She had more than lots of girls did.

Barb bustled around the small space and Joann scooted out of the way, coming to rest against the wall.

Ignoring the fact that Barb had literally backed her into a corner, Joann reasserted her big sister role by saying, "I don't want you overdoing. It's not every day my baby sister has a baby."

Barb's hard expression melted into softness and she touched her chest over her heart, delicate fingers splayed, but her eyes remained bone dry.

She'd decided to get on her feet and, like Joann, could dredge up steel resolve.

"I'll see you in a few days at most." Barb pointed to the food. "And those neighbors you dragged me to meet will be checking in." She grimaced, an overdone caricature. "Thanks for that. Not that I'm not grateful for meals."

Joann couldn't help but grin. The neighbor lady had no children, was from North Carolina, and starved for company. Plus, she loved to cook. An answer to prayer if Joann had ever seen one.

"I'll be fine," Barb insisted.

Joann sobered. For reasons she couldn't explain, Joann couldn't quite believe her, but she gave in.

CHAPTER TWENTY-TWO

Seven days before Thanksgiving, Joann woke in her own bed for the first time in weeks, and from the moment the store opened, business kept her hopping. Though she hated to admit it, Barb had been right about Dad needing help.

To Joann's grateful relief, Mrs. Delarue came in to work, but ten minutes after arriving she dropped a bag of flour and it burst open. A cloud of white dusted the floor, products on a nearby bottom shelf, and Mrs. Delarue herself. In tears, the woman fled toward the back.

With no hesitation, Joann followed the distraught Mrs. Delarue while calling, "Dad! Take the register." Scanning the store, she spotted his lifted hand, simultaneously catching his muffled, "Got it."

She found Mrs. Delarue in the stock room holding a hankie to her nose.

Lowering the hanky, Mrs. Delarue peered at Joann with watery eyes and croaked out, "I'm so sorry."

"No need to apologize. I'm sorry to have put so many hours on you these last weeks. Do you need to go home?" It wasn't the best day to pare back on help, but Mrs. Delarue had gone above and beyond their original agreement while Joann was at Barb's.

Mrs. Delarue shook her head. "I love helping. It makes me feel useful." At this, she welled up again. "I can't believe they won't give him leave for Thanksgiving."

Matty.

Mrs. Delarue's son was stationed stateside, but hadn't been for a visit. Leave was hard to come by. The Delarues had been to see him, but Joann knew it wasn't the same. Holidays were hard when part of the family was missing. Nothing could fill the hole absent loved ones left.

Joann almost mentioned surely they'd see him for Christmas, barely stopping herself in time. Anything could happen by then. Nothing was guaranteed.

What must it be like, surrounded by constant reminders of happy family gatherings when her son wasn't home?

A vivid memory of spitballs hitting the back of her neck popped into mind. She hadn't always gotten on with Matty, but that didn't matter now, him being far from home and his mother.

Joann should send him a letter. If she sent a Christmas package, what kind of things should she include? She'd ask, but not right now.

Joann straightened her spine and grasped Mrs. Delarue by the shoulders. "I do need you. But I also need you rested. Today won't be the busiest day." Joann shook her finger with mock sternness. "I can't do without you on the busiest days, so I'm sending you home to put your feet up. Next week will be a madhouse."

Mrs. Delarue produced a weak smile. "All right. If you get in a pinch, call me."

"Yes, ma'am. I will."

Appearing sapped of energy, Mrs. Delarue collected her purse and shrugged on her coat. She left with it unbuttoned and hanging crooked.

Joann nibbled at a hangnail. Maybe she'd made things worse by sending Mrs. Delarue away, but she didn't have long to dwell on the issue.

A young woman came into the store, two toddlers in her wake. "Excuse me. Where are the buggies?"

Joann swiped at her hair. She should've put it in a ponytail earlier. "I'll find one, ma'am."

Shoppers in a hurry had left buggies near the front, not quite in the designated area at the entrance. Abandoned carts waited along the front of the store like discarded toys left by a messy child.

Joann retrieved a cart for the lady and then returned to the rest, nesting one inside and pushing them to the corral near the front door.

Before another customer could ask for help, she strode to the hall near the storeroom, where she'd left a box full of canned peas. Hefting it, she carried it to the main floor.

"What are you doing?" Nathan wheeled the dolly over and wrested the box from her. "Didn't you tell me to use the dolly to carry more than a few cans?" Taking on a mock teacher pose, hands on hips, he looked down his nose at her.

Distracted by her mental to-do list and out of sorts after being gone for almost two weeks, Joann wasn't in the mood for joking. "I was in a hurry. We have so much to do." She planted her fists in the small of her back and tried to massage the knotted muscles without being obvious.

"We'll get it done. Don't worry."

She didn't want to depend on Nathan for more than one reason. Plus, how could she prove herself if he constantly rescued her?

"I'm not worried. But you can use the dolly to take these over to the canned goods. Set them on the floor and I'll get them out. I have to check the coolers anyway." Without waiting for a reply, she continued through the store, taking mental inventory as she approached the front counter. Her intention was to check on her dad.

Three customers waited in line as he pecked at the register with one finger. White tape encircled his hand, covering the cut he'd gotten slicing ham. His fingers trembled. Over the years, the tremor brought on by fatigue had shown itself more frequently. No doubt her absence had burdened him.

Mrs. May, a long-time customer, came in, her face drawn and pale. Times were tight for the family, with Mr. May losing another job. Unlike the customers who stopped and chatted with other shoppers, Mrs. May walked straight to the produce section and picked over the discounted pumpkins. She selected a misshapen pumpkin and held it in her arms, but it began to slip, and Joann rushed to her side.

"Here, let me get that for you. Expecting a crowd this Thanksgiving?"

What a thoughtless question. Joann kicked herself. The family could barely feed themselves, much less company.

"Just us," Mrs. May said. The twins, a boy and a girl, had to be twelve or thirteen by now.

"Is there anything else you need?"

The woman blinked absently, her eyes roving the store. "I don't think so, dear."

"We'll be open until seven tonight, and tomorrow hours are seven to seven. I'll put this by the register for you." Joann carried the pumpkin, walking slowly, not rushing Mrs. May. The woman clutched her purse, her steps uncertain. She navigated the store as if it were a strange landscape, not the well-known place she'd frequented for years.

Joann put the pumpkin on the counter and leaned toward her father. "Dad, why don't we give Mrs. May the special Thanksgiving discount? For loyal customers."

His cloudy eyes peered at her from beneath knitted brows. Joann met his gaze straight on and his expression cleared.

Without any exchange of words, he caught her meaning, and greeted Mrs. May with a gentle, "Happy Thanksgiving, Mrs. May."

He rang her up, charging half the marked down price.

Joann opened a small paper bag, slid in a few loose sticks of gum and candies, and passed it to Mrs. May. "For the kids."

The woman flushed. "Oh, no. I couldn't."

"I'll have to throw them out if you don't take them. They're wrapped but not in the original package, and I can't let Dad eat too much candy. Bad for him, you know."

Mrs. May studied the toes of her scuffed shoes. "Thank you." Without looking up, she took the bag and the pumpkin.

A teenage boy, tall and gawky, knocked over a cardboard turkey advertisement for broth and Joann dashed over. "I've got it."

"I'm really sorry," the boy squeaked out.

"It's only cardboard." Joann propped up the turkey. "No harm done."

The boy, his neck as red as the turkey's wattle, continued to the bread section.

In ten years, the teen boy poking at her loaves of bread too hard might be away from home for the holidays.

Like Matty.

Earlier, she'd heard the old men talking around the checker table. Troops might be in Vietnam for ten years or more.

Nathan hadn't said if he was volunteering.

When they'd been younger, they'd talked about everything, ventured into deep and serious conversations. It was different when you were an adult. Talking about the future took on a whole different meaning during times of war—and when you were afraid of lending your heart. If it were battered too many times, it might stop beating.

She turned away, intent on finding work to distract her from her disturbing thoughts, and crashed into Nathan. He didn't say anything, merely cradled her elbows, steadying her. She wanted to press her face into his flannel shirt and cry for Mrs. May, and Matty Delarue, and the teenage boy ruining her bread, but most of all for Nathan, and if she were honest, for herself, because she was afraid sooner or later, he'd have to go. She didn't need him for the store, but she needed him. Or at least she thought she did.

She felt so firm in what she wanted for the store, and how she wanted to carve out a name for herself, yet uncertain about how to go about it and have Nathan too.

CHAPTER TWENTY-THREE

Church always had potluck after service on the Wednesday preceding Thanksgiving Day.

The TV was on as Dad waited for Joann to get ready. She wished he'd leave it off and take a break from the news. Another 240 American servicemen had been killed in the war during the space of a week, raising the total number of casualties to 1,335 dead, and over 6,000 wounded, a fast jump. The somber announcement had been the topic of conversation everywhere.

Joann slipped on a wide headband and patted her shiny nose with a smidge of powder before applying rose lipstick. Traces of lint clung to her orange skirt and she gave it a quick brush before heading downstairs.

Dad drove the sedan. Joann rode in the passenger seat holding a potato casserole wrapped in a dishtowel. On behalf of the store, they'd donated rolls and a sliced ham, already delivered, but Joann never liked to arrive empty-handed to a church dinner.

Neither of them talked during the drive. Light rain spat at the windshield, and the hiss of tires on pavement was a lonesome sound, adding to Joann's dreary mood.

Barb wouldn't be at the church tonight. Her absence felt like the missing harmony of a two-part song. Joann would see Barb and Charles at the house tomorrow, but lately life seemed easily shattered. Joann craved moments with her family.

Dad pulled into the church parking lot and found a spot.

"Full up today," he said.

Craning her neck, Joann scanned the lot for Nathan. "I guess Nathan and his dad aren't here yet."

He'd been around the store less these days, doing double time working the farm and fixing up his dad's house.

"Stay put." The keys jingled as Dad removed them from the ignition and said, "I'll come around."

At her door he took the pan, set it on the roof of the car, and helped her out.

"Thanks." Joann smoothed her skirt and retrieved the casserole. "I'll go pop this into the fellowship hall and see you in the church."

Near the sanctuary entrance, two boxes of white tapers sat on a table, candles for a prayer vigil.

Nathan approached and she felt relieved to see him. A silly thought. Where else would he be?

He didn't greet her, but picked out two candles and said, his tone somber, "Let's go sit."

She followed him to a pew near the back. Dad, though muted, greeted people. The silent drive to the church had recharged him enough to be his public self, at least for a while. Before long, he came and sat by Joann and Nathan.

Joann whispered to Nathan. "Couldn't get your dad to come?"

He shook his head. "Not even the temptation of food could persuade him tonight."

"I'm sorry." She squeezed his arm.

The sermon was short and the prayer time long.

***

By noon on Thanksgiving, the sun had shown up, turning the day toasty.

Joann had taken special care with the settings, ironing an ecru tablecloth and using the blue-flowered china. The silver remained buried in the cabinet, waiting for the polishing rag, and the lack of silver bothered Joann. It had been up to her to stitch together their days with tradition, but without an extra set of hands, the polishing never got done. Plain flatware it was.

A burst of laughter came from the small den on the other side of the house where Dad kept his books. He jokingly referred to it as his library. Dad's magazines would've taken over the whole house if she hadn't relegated them to his library long ago.

Barb sat on the couch in the living room, the baby tucked in a basket at her feet. Frowning, she plucked at her dress. "I can't believe how big I am."

"Don't be silly. You've scarcely had time to get over giving birth."

Barb rested her head on the back of the couch. She'd muss her hair, but Joann stopped herself from saying so.

Eyes closed, Barb said, "It feels like forever. I thought I'd be able to wear my regular clothes by now."

Joann sat beside her sister. A faint odor of sour milk clung to Barb.

Joann said, "I have zero advice or knowledge about how long it takes to get your figure back, but it can't be long. I see women with new babies all the time, and they seem fine. Don't worry about it."

Without lifting her head from the couch, Barb shot Joann a death glare. "Easy for you to say. You're not wearing a tent."

"You're right."

During the weeks living with a post-baby Barb, Joann had learned to agree, but she couldn't wait for her sister to return to normal.

Barb pulled a face. "I'm sorry, Jo. It's a lot different from what I thought it would be. Don't mind me."

A sad Barb was worse than a crabby Barb. Joann would have to think of something to cheer her up, and hope she'd bounce back soon.

The timer for the turkey dinged, prompting Joann to hop up. "Let me check on dinner."

The turkey emerged from the oven perfectly browned. Joann placed it on a platter and took it to the table.

Barb wandered into the kitchen. "What can I do?"

"Set out the tea and water pitchers, would you?"

While Barb fixed drinks, Joann ferried food to the table, a meal heavy on canned foods, but it made for a pretty presentation.

At the entrance of Dad's library, Joann hesitated. Dim lighting and dark paneling marked it as male territory.

Instead of entering, she raised her voice. "Dad? Charles? Dinner's ready."

Susan wailed.

Startled, Joann turned to see Barb bent over the baby, attempting to shush her.

In a hushed tone, Joann said, "I'm sorry. I shouldn't have been so loud."

"It doesn't matter." Barb ground the heel of her hand into her forehead. "She always wakes when it's time for us to sit down to dinner." She picked up the baby, snugging her close. "Come on, Susie. Let's go warm a bottle." Sighing, Barb said, "It's not time for her scheduled feeding yet, but if I wait, she'll scream down the house."

Charles and Dad came to the table, all smiles. They got along well. Dad calling him son was as natural as could be, but it didn't help the insecurities Joann had entertained her whole life.

If she'd been a boy, Dad wouldn't think her incapable, now would he?

Jealousy flared and bitterness coated her tongue. She swallowed it down. None of it was Charles's fault. She couldn't even stay mad at Dad, because he was a good father. The best.

He simply couldn't see her as a person who could manage the store.

Banishing her negative thoughts, she asked Charles about his car, a topic he loved.

As soon as Barb came in with baby and bottle, Charles hopped up. "Here, honey." He held out her chair.

"Thank you." Barb sat and popped the bottle into Susie's eager mouth.

Dad picked up the carving knife. "Is this sharp?"

He didn't wait for an answer. Instead, he went to the kitchen. Banging noises ensued, then the *scritch, scritch* of blade against sharpener. Barb and Joann cut their eyes at one another, expressions caught between amusement and exasperation.

At least Dad didn't bring the sharpener to the table.

Charles looked from one to another. "What?"

Joann scooted her chair up and pitched her voice low. "He always has to sharpen it, no matter what."

Barb jiggled the baby in her lap. "It's a thing."

"I see."

Clearly, Charles didn't.

Wielding the knife as if going into battle, Dad returned to the table and stabbed the turkey. The knife stuck out at an angle.

The momentary alarm on Charles's face almost set Joann giggling, and she didn't dare look at Barb.

Dad took his seat at the head of the table. "Let's pray."

He gave thanks, and they passed the bowls of food.

Charles said, "How's record sales?"

Joann's face burned, but she answered. "Good."

Several local groups had made records, sparking interest. They'd sold more of the popular singles too. According to Nathan, the reception of her idea to carry local groups had been encouraging. But Dad hadn't said a word.

Charles turned to her dad. "Joann is one smart cookie. You should be proud of her."

Dad jabbed at a potato with his fork. "Never said I wasn't."

While not exactly forbidding, the atmosphere became dense. The hard slats in the back of Joann's chair rubbed against her spine.

Charles seemed to sense the mood and switched his attention to Barb. Her plate bore a lone slice of turkey breast Dad had placed there. Charles took this as a cue to heap her plate.

She protested, "That's too much! It'll go to waste."

"We can take it home." Charles continued spooning servings of sweet potatoes and green beans.

Instead of standing her ground the way she usually did, Barb retreated into herself, concentrating on the baby. The meal progressed as she awkwardly attempted one-handed eating. Charles cut her meat for her.

Joann inwardly cringed, thinking he would've done better to take the baby.

Quiet resignation flattened Barb's character. Joann didn't like it. Or the unease making her heart pound. Her mouthful of turkey went down dry, and she followed it with a gulp of water. Everyone had eaten more than Barb had been able to manage holding the baby. Susan had taken half the bottle and Barb positioned the baby upright to burp.

Joann stroked the baby's back, then, with the same lightness, tucked Barb's hair behind her ear. "Can I take her?"

Without waiting for an answer, Joann lifted the baby and took the bottle, amazed at her own efficiency. The short time she'd helped care for the child must have imprinted skills. Joann pointed her chin at Barb's plate. "You eat." She kissed the baby's head and jostled her. "And you eat too. After you bring up air."

A chuckle went around the table.

Joann held the baby, burped her, and fed her the rest of the bottle. By then, Barb had picked over her food, leaving the majority on her plate. She reclaimed the baby. Little Susan whined and flung her tiny, clenched fists.

As the men moved into the living room, Joann heard Dad say, "Fancy a game?"

He'd found a chess table and set it up, polishing the wooden pieces until they shone. Of course Charles agreed.

Joann whispered, "Is Charles any good at chess?"

Barb lifted her shoulders. She got up and paced around the table, jiggling Susan, and the baby quieted.

Joann put the cover on the bowl of potatoes and stacked the plates.

Swaying side to side, Barb continually rubbed the baby's back. "I'll help in a minute, as soon as I get her down."

"No need. I've got it."

As quietly as she could, Joann finished clearing the dirty dishes. She left them on the counter and returned. The empty baby bottle sat on the table and Barb walked the room, baby Susan tucked next to her neck.

Joann stopped her and peered at the baby. She whispered, "She's out like a light. Let's go put her to bed."

In Barb's old room, they settled the sleeping baby on a quilt and tiptoed down the stairs.

Barb stepped toward the dining room.

Joann stopped her. "Leave it. I want to show you something in the store."

"What if Susan wakes?"

"There are two capable men here. If she wakes, one can come fetch us while the other stays here. We'll be right across the street."

"But..."

"It'll only take a minute."

Joann left the food on the table, notifying the men where they were going.

Eyes glued to the game, Dad moved his rook. "What about pie? We haven't had dessert yet."

Joann dropped a kiss on the top of his head. "We'll have it after dinner's had time to settle." She turned to Barb and grinned. "Come on, Sis."

Leaving the mess felt glorious, and she wasn't about to let Dad keep her from her mission.

The girls entered the store and with each step they took, the floorboards creaked in greeting.

Barb looked over her shoulder as if she had long-distance x-ray vision and could see her baby. "What did you want to show me, anyway?"

"A new dress."

Barb scowled. "What are you talking about?"

"Oh, don't be a stick-in-the-mud. You don't like the dress you're wearing, and we have racks of clothes here."

"Racks? Of what? Overalls and flannel shirts?"

"We have sweaters and tops too. At least one rack. What's the point of owning a store if we can't go shopping in it from time to time? Look, Barb. I want to give you a new outfit. Don't spoil my fun. Come on."

Joann ran up the staircase, the time-worn handrail smooth against her palm. The old store felt as secure as a hug from an old auntie, welcoming and generous. The delicious sensation of doing something she oughtn't overtook Joann.

She went straight to the shirt she'd thought of, an orange and brown A-line with cream trim around the neck and long sleeves. It would fit Barb, for certain. A lightweight cream sweater would pair with it perfectly, and Joann found one hanging on the rack. She dangled the selections in front of a reluctant Barb.

"Better than long johns," she sing-songed, waggling the clothes on their hangers.

Barb barely cracked a smile.

"Come on, try them on."

"All right."

As she'd expected, both fit Barb, and her sister made the clothes lovely. Joann insisted they find a headband to match.

Joann clipped a bow into Barb's hair.

Barb said, "It's harder than I thought it would be."

Not speaking, Joann waited, trying a different bow, playing with Barb's hair.

"I'm tired all the time. And Charles treats me like a child. You saw him. Cutting my food, for Pete's sake! I don't like him taking over instead of asking me what I need help with and then I feel stupid for feeling upset. What's wrong with me?"

"Nothing's wrong with you."

"He's only trying to help."

"Tell him how you feel. But in a nice way." Joann put back all except two of the bows.

The gentle teasing didn't produce the usual retort, so Joann turned earnest.

"It's plain to see Charles loves you. Tell him what you're feeling and thinking." Joann twisted a strand of Barb's hair. "It'll be all right. It'll pass." She let go of Barb's hair and it untwisted into a loose coil. "And call me if you need me."

Barb grabbed Joann's hand and squeezed. "I will." She pasted on a wobbly smile. "You're right. It'll pass, I'm sure."

Joann prayed it did.

Back at the house, the girls found Charles in Dad's recliner, feet propped and snoring. It would appear Barb wasn't the only one tired, but Joann didn't point it out. Better to bite her tongue in this case.

Barb cocked her head to the side and examined Charles, her expression vacillating between dark disapproval and tenderness. Tenderness won. She draped an afghan over his legs, and then ascended the stairs. Joann searched the downstairs for Dad but he wasn't there. The overhead floorboards creaked, accompanied by off-key, tenor singing.

Curious, Joann mounted the stairs. Barb was on the landing near the bedroom's open door. She brought a finger to her upturned lips. Joann inched closer. Dad held a wide-eyed Susan, his back curved over the baby protectively as he rocked her in his big arms and crooned a verse from "Baby Love."

He turned around. He didn't start at seeing them, but looked sheepish. "Your music wearing off on me."

With infinite care, he put Susan in Barb's arms and then kissed Barb on the cheek. "You bring her back to see her old grandpa anytime. She likes me well enough, and I can keep her occupied."

After Barb and Charles left, Dad said, "How about we have some coffee?"

"Are you sure? It'll keep you awake."

"Milk and pie, then." He stuck both hands in his pockets and wandered into the living room. Joann frowned. She didn't like cleaning crumbs from the carpets.

Joann cut the pie, a sliver for her and a larger piece for Dad, and brought the plates with her. He sat bent forward, elbows on knees.

"Here you go, Dad."

Taking the proffered plate, he looked at her with a hangdog expression. "Jo, you know I'm proud of you, right?"

Tears sprang to her eyes. She shrugged. "I don't know."

He set the plate down on his knee and toyed with the fork. "You've done so much for the store. The community. I can see that. But don't you want more from life than slaving away in the store?"

Joann perched on the edge of the couch. "It's more than a job to me. Don't you feel it, Dad? Where would people go if they needed medicine, or a friendly face? Isn't being a trustworthy and steady presence for the community what you've always wanted for Kincaid's?"

"That's fine for me, but I don't want you giving your whole life to the family business purely because it's all you know. And I don't want you shouldering it alone when I'm gone." He scratched the fringe of hair at the back of his head. "I never should've burdened you with such a responsibility. I see that now, and it's the whole reason I wanted to sell."

"Wanted to?"

Dad sighed. "You're a stubborn one, Jo."

Takes one to know one.

Joann held in her snort.

"I won't sell as long as you want me to keep the store."

Joann sucked in a breath.

"But you have to promise me something."

"What?"

"Promise me you'll think about what your future could be and what you really want. Don't tie yourself to this old place because of duty."

Later, Joann put on a faded blue apron and busied herself cleaning the dishes, mulling over Dad's words. And her own.

The advice she'd given Barb was solid. Tell him how you feel, straight from the heart. She'd done just that with Dad. She should take her own advice and hash it out with Nathan. It sounded so easy. But what did she feel? Confused. Unsure. Scared. Of what?

Was she unsure of Nathan's feelings for her or unsure if she wanted to be married?

A wife didn't work full-time away from husband and home. It simply wasn't done, but she couldn't see giving up being a Kincaid. Running the store was in her blood, and she'd loved it since the first day she'd been allowed to ring up a purchase. Her ten-year-old self had felt so grown up, so perfectly right behind the register. It felt like her true place.

Thoughts tumbled about her mind as she washed the dishes and sponged the countertop. *Mrs. Canfield's Cookery Book* sat there, though she hadn't used it for this dinner, only intended to.

She opened the book. On the page in front of her, a faded line of ink cited Proverbs 3: 5-6, the very scripture she passed every day when she went out the door. She paused. Without the usual feelings of guilt, Joann took the scripture at face value. Look to God, and His word, and He would guide her.

It felt like a promise.

Joann didn't put much truck in signs, but God could certainly use a cookbook to speak to her. She couldn't suppress a wry half smile.

All right, then.

After she'd prayed over it, she called Nathan and asked him to be at the store in the morning before they opened. She kept the conversation light, told him she needed help with some small repairs, which was true enough.

If the time seemed right, she'd talk to him then.

CHAPTER TWENTY-FOUR

The next morning, Joann arrived at the store an hour early and let Nathan in. Practice conversations tumbled around her mind as he climbed a wooden ladder and hammered fresh framing trim inside the perimeter of the front store window. Outside, a steady drizzle saturated the pine trees near the road. Dankness permeated the walls of the store, turning the interior damp.

Nathan slipped the hammer into the loop of his overalls. "Can you hand me up the last piece of trim?"

She did so, and he finished the job.

Pleased, Joann stepped back to take in the whole window. "It's ready for paint."

"What brought on this sudden need to spruce up the place?" Nathan stepped down from the last rung of the ladder.

"Advent is a week away." Joann picked up a quart of paint she'd left on the counter and jiggled it. "To tell the truth, I've put off minor upkeep."

"You're way too hard on yourself. I think looking after Barb and the baby counts as an excellent excuse."

"I suppose I could always find excuses." But she wouldn't. Great-grandma Lacey had managed, and so would she. Joann lifted her chin. "I'll catch up."

He took the can from her.

She fidgeted with the hem of her sleeve. "I confess it's been harder than I expected. Discouraging at times. The worst was when I found out Dad had been thinking of selling the store." Joann shuddered.

The slight widening of his eyes disappeared in a flash. If she didn't know him well, she would've missed his surprise.

The paint can clunked as he set it on the windowsill.

"Had been?"

"He's promised not to, now. We've come to an understanding. He gets how I feel about the store."

"And how is that?" Brows knit in puzzlement, Nathan cocked his head to the side.

Did he really not know after all this time?

"Nathan, I want to always work at the store. Run it, actually."

Blank-faced, he asked, "And where does that leave me?"

Joann swallowed hard. Insecurity froze her tongue, yet she had to speak up. If Nathan truly wanted to be with her, he would take all of her. Being the storekeeper at Kincaid's Mercantile was a big part of who she was.

She licked her lips. "I guess it's up to you. I don't want you to give up your dream, but I can't see myself being happy if I weren't serving in my community, and I truly believe my calling is here. I was born for this."

"That's it, then? You'll never be happy being a wife and mother?"

"That's not what I said. I know I'd be happy with you. I've never wanted any other man. You're my best friend." She scrubbed at her forehead, then clasped her trembling hands together in a tight knot. Should she bring up her fears about the war? Maybe not now. Stick with defining their relationship first. "Although I'm a little scared about having a child. I always thought I wanted kids, but I wonder if something's wrong with me. When I hold Susan, I love her, but nothing like the love I feel for Barb or Dad, or you. What if I'm no good with babies?"

She held her breath. If Nathan ignored her, told her she'd feel differently once she had her own baby, or said she was being silly, she'd have to let him go. It was important for him to understand her. As much as it hurt, she'd have to put an end to things if he disregarded her.

But he didn't.

"I always imagined you'd live at the farm with me and we'd have kids. I never thought about how that meant you'd have to give up the store. Obviously, I know you love working here, but... I want a family, Jo. With you. I don't want anyone else, but I don't see how we can work things out."

He seemed ready to cry, and Joann could barely look at him. This was a grief they couldn't comfort each other through.

He said, "Let's think about it awhile."

It hurt to breathe. Even though she knew she'd been right—the conversation had been needed—she wanted to reel her words back in and restart the day. Joann fought the urge to throw herself into his arms and bury her face in his shirt. She knew his smells. Soap and toothpaste, because she hadn't made coffee yet or given him a pastry, and she longed to kiss him and forget all about how their worlds didn't want to line up.

"How long is a while?"

"I don't know. I feel like you've been stringing me along." He tugged at his ear. "Not that I blame you. I was the one who wanted freedom after high school." He grimaced.

Quick to get beyond the past to the here and now, Joann said, "We were kids back then, and neither one of us ready for a forever commitment." She reached for him and touched his arm. "And I wasn't stringing you along, I was just scared and unsure."

Nathan raked his hands through his hair. "Listen, it's better we think about all this before we say anything else right now. I should go."

"Will you come back later?"

"I don't know, Jo." His face bunched up as if he'd broken a bone. "I thought... I don't know what I thought."

Tears came to Joann's eyes.

"I'll talk to you later." He dropped a kiss on her head. "Promise."

She clung to those words and let him go.

***

Instead of obsessing about Nathan, Joann tried to focus on transitioning from Thanksgiving to Christmas. Barb had always handled the decorations, a task Joann hadn't appreciated enough. Paper turkeys, cornucopias, and seasonal items turned up in unexpected places no matter how many times Joann searched them out.

Waiting on Nathan to figure out what he wanted was torture and she wondered if that's how he'd felt these last months.

She didn't like it.

No two people could be friends for as long as she and Nathan without having had occasional separations and even ugly fights, but they'd always found their way back to each other.

She hoped they could do so now.

At least the store kept her busy. She checked and double-checked stock, and wrote an advertisement for the paper touting the records made by local groups as the perfect Christmas gift. Sales continued to surprise her. The pressure was off, now she and Dad had an understanding, but the sales boost couldn't hurt.

None of it helped. She missed Nathan.

On Thursday, near closing time, Dad had already gone to the house with a stomach complaint, and Joann asked Mrs. Delarue if she could stay an hour longer.

"Sorry, dear. I need to get home. Mr. Delarue needs his supper. What did you need?"

"Just unpacking Christmas decorations. But what I can't do on my own will wait." Joann smiled, hoping her loneliness didn't bleed through. In truth, she didn't need much help at all, but didn't want to unravel tinsel and unpack jolly Santas alone.

Mrs. Delarue plucked at her shopkeeper apron, still as clean as when she'd donned it earlier in the afternoon. "Are you sure?"

"I'm sure."

Mrs. Delarue clasped her hands in front of her stomach and twisted her fingers. She looked like a worried hen. "I can't come in tomorrow. I have my eye appointment."

"Yes. It's on the calendar."

"Why don't you call Nathan?" Mrs. Delarue's eyes lit up. "I'm sure he wouldn't mind helping decorate."

Joann bobbed her head, unable to reply past the boulder stuck in her throat.

After Mrs. Delarue hung up her apron and went off to see to her husband's supper, Joann flipped the open sign to closed.

In the quiet of the empty store, she turned on the radio for company and caught the middle of a news broadcast. They were talking about the March on Washington for Peace in Vietnam, the biggest demonstration so far, with almost 35,000 participants, organized by the Committee for a SANE Nuclear Policy.

Her mind spun like a pinwheel caught in a strong wind. She didn't know if she wanted to run to Nathan to talk about the crumbling world, or run to him to hide from it. In either case, she felt his absence sorely.

When the program ended, she snapped the radio off but wasn't ready to tackle the storeroom. The job wasn't a big deal, as far as effort, but she'd never done it alone. She went into the office and straight to the black phone and dialed Barb.

On the second ring, Barb picked up. "Hello?"

This time Joann didn't feel her sister out to get a sense of her mood before speaking. "I need you to come over Sunday after church. I can't decorate the store without you. Say you'll come."

Barb sighed. "All right."

"Thank you."

"You don't sound yourself. Did you want to tell me something else?"

Joann shook her head as if Barb could see her. "Not right now."

A sympathetic cluck came through the line. "I'm not sure how much work I can do with Susan along." At Barb's weary tone, the spike of concern Joann felt every time she talked to her sister dug in a little deeper.

Joann said, "I'm sure we'll manage. Besides, Dad will want to watch Susan. He'll be more help with the baby than he'll ever be with decorating."

"That's the truth." A note of pride crept into Barb's voice. "He's gaga for her. We'll be there. Maybe with bells on, but don't hold me to it."

"Thanks, sissy."

They hung up.

When Barb came, they'd have cocoa with marshmallows and play Christmas music while they worked. It would cheer them both.

While not exactly humming carols, Joann crossed the street to home with lighter footsteps.

She found Dad in his undershirt watching television.

"Not feeling any better?"

Dad let his head loll on the back of the chair. "Sorry, Jo."

She patted his arm. "No need to be sorry. Do you have a fever?"

"I don't know. Can you go find a thermometer?"

He gazed at her like a wounded creature, helpless to search the medicine cabinet, and her happiness faded. She almost snapped at him to go find one himself.

Be kind. He can't help being sick.

Although he could've monitored his own temperature.

She swallowed her frustration. "Back in a minute."

Once she gave him the thermometer and fetched him a glass of lemonade, heavy on the ice, he mumbled, "You're so good to me."

The last of her irritation melted.

"Someone's got to look after you," she scolded gently, tucking a blanket over his lap.

The red of the thermometer climbed to one hundred.

"You have a fever." She shook the thermometer down as if she might fling the mercury right out of the tip. It wasn't a good time to be short of workers in the store. Mrs. Delarue was unavailable, and the other help was after school only.

Which meant she must call Nathan. He'd come. Her head told her heart not to get excited, but she couldn't help it. She wanted to see him.

CHAPTER TWENTY-FIVE

Friday morning Joann opened the store alone, put the coffee on, and brought the newspapers in. The regulars showed up, as expected, as did shoppers.

A few minutes before ten, Nathan strode though the door. "Where's Mrs. Delarue? Didn't you have help opening?"

"It was fine. I handled it."

He scowled. "Next time, call me and I'll come earlier."

Like her customers would want to see *that* happy face. Joann bit back the sour comment. The morning had been busy, and a headache had dug in. This wasn't the reunion she'd hoped for. She forced a smile. "Thanks for coming in."

His expression softened. "Are you all right? You look peaked."

Just like that, sweet Nathan was back, turning her mushy inside.

Maybe the kindness covered bad news.

And just like that, her mood shifted back again. Acid burned the back of her throat.

What if he'd decided marriage wasn't a great idea if she remained committed to the store?

One by one, she tugged on her fingers until the knuckles popped. "A little tired, and a little worried about Dad." *And about you.*

"What's going on with him?"

"Actually, a fever, but not a bad one. Hopefully, it will go away soon, and he'll be back to himself." As long as an illness didn't knock him down for long. Or send him into a depression.

"I can read you like a book, you know," Nathan said. "You really should've called me to come in earlier. I wish you'd let me help more." He took a step toward her, stopping an arm's length away.

It felt like miles.

He continued, "I've been thinking about us. Are you sure you want a future running the store all by yourself?"

By herself?

Joann's stomach plummeted to her feet, but then sudden peace blanketed her as she took in the sad slope of his eyes and the paleness of his face. Perhaps his question wasn't an ultimatum.

Joann inhaled. "I want to prove I can make something of myself, same as you do. Is it so hard to understand I need to do this on my own? For myself? For my family?"

"I guess not. If you put it like that. You've always been a leader." A smile twitched the corner of his mouth, but it slid off before taking hold. "It's not realistic for me to expect you to give up something you feel called to."

"If I could change, I would. But I can't see it."

"No kids." He stated as a fact, his face unreadable.

"I didn't say that!" Joann huffed. Why did he put words in her mouth? Instead of reacting, she reached for a prayer and reclaimed her footing. "I said I was scared. What if I'm not the mothering sort?"

Nathan drew back, his chin nesting into his neck. "Are you kidding? You care for your family and every hurting person coming through the door."

The bell over the door sounded, the tinkle drowned out by the whining cry of a toddler. His mother dragged him inside with grim determination and proceeded to the canned vegetables aisle.

Nathan caught the sympathetic look Joann tossed the boy.

"See?" He said softly. "Heart of gold."

Joann blinked back tears.

He said, "I've been thinking about where to go from here, about us."

"So have I."

He stepped closer, putting a finger to her lips. "Let me finish."

Joann trembled. She'd been quiet for too long for all the wrong reasons, but she nodded.

"I want us to talk more."

"So do I." Joann sniffled and dabbed at her cheeks.

"We have to be on the same page, or able to agree to disagree." He rubbed his neck and wiped his palm across his jaw. "Can we take it slow and see where it goes?"

"Yes," she said. In case he didn't understand her, she added a vigorous nod. She didn't even care what he meant by taking it slow.

Anything would be better than the empty hole his absence would surely leave.

He shuffled his feet, then stuffed his hands into his pockets.

She cleared her throat. "I guess we'd better tend to our work."

"Sure thing, boss."

She would wait and see. And pray like her future depended on it.

***

On Advent Sunday, Barb and Charles attended church with Joann and Dad. The call to worship began and they stood in their pew. Halfway through the first verse, Dad stepped into the aisle to shake Nathan's hand. He'd come in late.

Nathan shifted his gaze from the spot next to Joann to meet her eyes, questioning. He wanted to sit with her.

Dad displayed a sudden fascination with the stained-glass windows, as if he'd never noticed the array of colors before.

Barb gave Joann a nudge, breaking the frozen moment, and Joann smiled. The family shuffled and rearranged, creating a space in the pew. Nathan ended up squashed between Joann and her dad. If they'd been alone, he might have taken her hand. Or not. They still had much to talk about, but his presence beside her warmed her to the core, and her stomach did baby flips.

He bent close to her ear and whispered, "I brought a tiny tree for the store window, and evergreen wreaths."

So, he wanted to tell her about decorations for the store. Joann deflated inside but nailed her smile in place.

During the service, Joann struggled to pay attention to the pastor.

The last notes of the benediction hadn't faded before Barb gripped her sleeve. "I need to get Susan down for a nap. Let's get over to the house." Her eyes tracked a trio of older ladies heading their way.

If the girls didn't hurry, the baby-hungry women would smother Barb with good wishes and Susan with unwanted cuddles.

"Come on, then." Joann circumvented the well-wishers by poking Charles in the back and almost barreling over him. "Baby needs her dinner. Come to the parking lot." Without waiting for a reply, she steered Barb out the side door and hustled to Charles's car.

The girls were situated in the back seat by the time Charles opened the driver's side door and stuck his head in. "Are you going to tell your dad you're leaving?"

Joann waved a hand in the air. "He'll figure it out."

Dad, busy chatting it up with churchgoers, wouldn't care one iota.

"Let's go." Joann tucked her skirt close to her legs.

Barb nestled Susan into her lap and rested her head on Joann's shoulder. So tired. The weight on her shoulder reminded Joann of long ago road trips when she had always been her sister's pillow.

She said, "Charles, do you have a blanket in here?"

Wearing a hang-dog expression, he shook his head.

Joann would bet ten dollars there would be one in the car for the next trip.

As they approached the Kincaid's white, two-story home, Joann said, "We need to change clothes at the house, but I figured since we're decorating the store today, we might as well have lunch over there. I left chili simmering in the cooker fryer in the break room."

Charles peered into the rearview mirror. "Sounds good."

Joann patted Barb. "Okay with you? Or would you rather stay at the house to feed Susan?" The dark circles under Barb's eyes had prompted Joann's offer of an excuse. The store had a rocker, but no place to lie down if Barb wanted a rest. Joann kicked herself for not considering it earlier. Motherhood had worn Barb to a nub.

"The store is fine." Barb wore a wistful expression. "It'll be like old times."

A quiet baby Susan curled against Barb's chest, her tiny body relaxed, save for a starfish hand opening and closing as she blinked serious eyes at the world. She didn't even fuss when Barb passed her to Charles.

Barb headed upstairs. "Let's hurry and change before she sets up wailing."

Joann kept one ear tuned for Dad. And Nathan. After all, he'd said he had a tree for the store. Unless he'd already dropped it off. Maybe she should've asked him to come over for lunch. What if he took her scooting out of church so fast the wrong way?

If Joann had been on her own, she would've walked across the street to the store no matter the weather, but that wouldn't work with a baby. They piled back into the car and headed over.

A small tree and two wreaths waited under the front awning. Her heart sank. She took a deep breath and gave herself a mental shake. No point in letting disappointment barge in. She had Barb, and the baby, and Charles, who she'd grown fond of. Dad on the way. More than a carful of blessings.

They parked around back of the store and got out of the car, Joann hurrying ahead to unlock the door. The key had barely slid into the lock when the rumble and backfire of a vehicle reached her ears. She spun around. Dad pulled up, followed by Nathan's truck, Old Bessie. Joann felt a grin almost split her face.

Charles huddled with Barb, shielding the baby between them. He said, "Joann? Need help with the lock?"

"Sorry." She fumbled with the key and opened the door. The good smell of warm food greeted them.

Dad and Nathan were on their heels and Dad rubbed his stomach. "Smells good!"

Joann lifted the lid to the cooker and gave the chili a stir. "Dad, could you get some saltines?" She hadn't had time to bake cornbread.

"Sure thing. Come on through, Nathan. Bring in the tree."

Joann hollered after them, "Stay and eat with us, Nathan." Now he was here she wasn't letting him get away. At least she could feed him.

Barb unpacked a bottle from Susan's diaper bag.

Joann reached for it. "Here, let me." She ran warm water into a dish, plopped the bottle in to warm, then found bowls and spoons for the chili, stacking them next to the cooker. After scooping instant tea into a pitcher, she added water in and stirred. Lunch was all set.

A pacing Barb jiggled Susan while Charles lurked near the wall, as out of place as a zebra at a horse show.

Joann took pity on him. "Why don't you go see what the guys are up to? Make sure Dad didn't get lost."

Susan had finished half her bottle before Dad returned with saltines and set them next to the cooker.

The room felt tight, full of people. Joann rather liked it. The visions she'd had of decorating a cold, empty store all on her lonesome evaporated like morning mist.

Dad rubbed his hands together. "I think it's time for the blessing, if the ladies say so."

Joann bowed her head, and the rest followed suit. Dad rumbled a prayer of thanks.

Barb shifted Susan to her shoulder and Joann extended her arms.

"Let me."

She took the burp cloth from Barb and flipped it across her own shoulder before placing Susan in the correct position and gently patting her back. She jerked her head toward the food.

"Eat." Her tone held mock sternness.

"What about you?"

"I'm going to rock my niece." Earlier, she'd set a wooden rocking chair near the big front window. She'd soak in the peace and quiet of the empty store. Joann kept her gaze on Barb's hazel eyes. "And Nathan will bring me a bowl of chili in a while." She didn't dare look his way.

The corner of Barb's mouth quirked up a fraction. "I'll see that he does."

"Thank you." If Joann had been wearing a skirt instead of pants, she would've swished them as she left.

The little tree and two wreaths sat near the front door, filling the store with the scent of pine and Christmas.

Joann hooked one of the rocker rails with her ankle and dragged the chair closer to the checkers table.

A wriggly Susan emitted a squeaky grumble. Cupping the baby's head, Joann scrunched her face in sympathy. "Hold on a minute."

Joann arranged herself and the baby in the chair and let Susan finish her bottle. Hustle-bustle days were Joann's favorite, but she loved the creak of floorboards as she rocked, and the low rumble of voices. Times like these she imagined her Great-great-grandpa behind the counter, trading and selling, then later, Great-grandma Lacey. How many people had come for supplies or news over the decades?

Footsteps approached, and Joann looked up. Nathan held a bowl with both hands, careful not to spill. Two feet away from her, he came to an uncertain stop.

"Put it on the table."

He did as she asked, eyeballing the baby with caution, the way one might approach a feral kitten. No matter how big or tough the man, when an infant was in the room, the little tyrant ruled.

She stifled a grin.

All innocence, Joann lifted the baby. "Want to hold her?"

Blanching, Nathan drew back. "She's so tiny."

"Here, let's switch."

Joann put the bottle on the table and got up. Every line of his body rigid, Nathan lowered himself into the rocker.

Without ceremony, Joann slid the baby into his arms and guided him to give the bottle. "When she's done, burp her right away. Don't let her suck air."

For a guy who claimed to want kids, he looked downright terrified of babies.

She stroked the baby's head and glanced at Nathan from under her eyelashes. "Thanks for bringing the tree and wreaths."

"I'll help you put them up."

Joann smiled at the promise.

She ate her chili, watching Nathan. He needed a haircut. It always bothered him when the ends of it curled into corkscrews and stuck in his shirt collar. High on his cheekbones, two patches of color glowed as he frowned in concentration.

What if he got drafted and never had a child? Her lungs froze, incapable of breathing.

Life could be so unfair.

A footstool rested nearby. She dragged it close to Nathan and sat, almost at his feet. "Will you enlist?"

Nathan didn't seem surprised by the question. "My dad. He wouldn't take that well."

"I imagine not."

Poor Mr. Poole who stayed away from July fireworks and didn't go hunting.

He stopped rocking. "And I wouldn't want to leave you."

Joann put her head on his knee. "What if God convicted you to go, what then?"

"I'd pray about it." He touched the crown of her head and she gazed up at him. "*We'd* pray about it."

What did he mean? Was he ready to accept her as she was and move ahead with a relationship? How could that happen? Too much was going on, at home and in the world.

Still, those deep brown eyes drew her in and she was helpless.

She said, "All right."

Later, when the rest of the group joined them, Dad switched on the radio behind the counter and Bing Crosby crooned Christmas cheer from the speaker. Charles claimed Susan and walked her back and forth. Now and then, the wooden floorboards creaked under his feet, the store approving, Joann fancied. She didn't bat the thought away with practical thinking as she normally would. The ancestors would've approved of Charles, she thought.

He passed by Joann, and she pointed to a basket she'd lined with a thick blanket. "If she nods off, tuck her in."

Susan blinked and crinkled up her tiny face.

Joann chuckled. "If she wants you to, that is."

Barb fingered the glass ornaments Joann had set out. "I'm not sure we should use these. Last year four of them got broken."

Joann said, "You're right."

Barb rewrapped them. "Save these for the house."

"I might get an aluminum tree for the house," Joann said. "They're so much easier. No needles, and no tinsel."

Nathan joined the girls and grunted. "What's wrong with tinsel?"

Dad clapped him on the back. "Nothing at all. And aluminum trees don't make the place smell like Christmas." He moseyed to the front window and surveyed the assortment of painted metal nutcrackers and angels Barb had arranged on white poly fluff. "That's real pretty, Barb. Can I borrow Joann for a minute?"

Barb put the last of the rejected ornaments into its box. "Don't leave me to finish this alone."

"She'll be back." He turned to Nathan. "I'd like for you to come to the office too."

Joann shot a look at Nathan, then Barb, whose eyebrows climbed halfway up her forehead. She shrugged.

Joann and Nathan followed Dad.

Humming along to "Silver Bells," Dad went straight to his desk and opened a side drawer, taking out a paper. He sat down heavily, sighing with contentment.

He was in a good mood. What was he up to?

"I wanted to talk to Joann about this, but since you're here, Nathan, it might interest you. I know you plan to restart and expand the orchard, so your reason for hanging around the store can't be a part-time job."

"Dad!" Joann's cheeks prickled, and she hazarded a glance at Nathan.

He seemed just as flustered, but held steady. "No sir, it's not."

Joann said, "Dad, my relationships are not your business. This isn't the dark ages." What was the document he had on the desk? Her dowry?

Dad put his hands up in surrender. "You're getting me wrong, Jo. Hear me out."

With great effort, Joann drew a shaky breath, concentrating on slowing her galloping pulse. "Go ahead, then."

Dad placed his finger in the center of the document on his desk. "First off, I know how you take things on, so hear me when I say I'm perfectly healthy."

Joann's outrage melted into confusion. "What are you talking about? Did you change your will?"

"My will hasn't changed. You and Barb each get an even share of everything. I simply added this letter of instruction."

"What does that have to do with Nathan? Shouldn't Barb be in here?"

"Barb knows about this and agreed it was only right. These are my wishes. It won't mean much in the eyes of the law, but it's how I feel." He rotated the paper and slid it toward Joann.

She picked it up and frowned at the small print. It was hard to give attention to the letter with Nathan's gaze boring into her and Dad waiting, but she read the words.

These are the instructions and wishes of Howard Henry Kincaid, Jr. regarding my business, Kincaid's Mercantile. Upon my death or mental incapacitation, I wish for complete control and assets of my business, Kincaid's Mercantile, to be handed over in whole to my eldest daughter, Joann Elizabeth Kincaid, to manage. If she is married, or becomes married, it is my wish she is to remain as the acting sole proprietor of Kincaid's Mercantile until such time as she decides otherwise. These are my wishes.

Signed,
Howard Henry Kincaid, Jr.
December 1965

Dad said, "I can't control the future, but I can leave a clear record of what I want done with the store." He furrowed his brow, then lifted one shoulder. "It doesn't mean much, I know."

In a flash, Joann scooted around the desk and hugged her dad tight. "It means everything."

He patted her arm. "You're strangling me, Jo."

Laughing, she disentangled herself. She said to Nathan, "He gave me the store."

Dad groused, "Not yet. Don't go changing anything." The grumpy effect was ruined when he tucked his thumbs into his suspenders and puffed out his chest, pleased with himself. Unable to hold a hint of a frown, he positively beamed at Joann.

A crooked smile appeared and disappeared on Nathan's broad face. "I'm lost. Care to clue me in? What's it say?"

With both hands, Joann held the letter toward Nathan as if it were breakable.

He took it and studied the words on the paper. Emotions kaleidoscoped across his features, and Joann tensed. She hadn't considered how he'd interpret this news.

A nasty little thought reared up in her mind.

Was this Dad warning Nathan off, just another way for Dad to control her? No. She rejected the idea. But did it appear so to Nathan?

He gave the letter back to her and cleared his throat. "Seems clear."

He pinned Dad with a look. Dad met his gaze straight on with no animosity, his expression transparent and untroubled.

Nathan scrubbed at his neck as if a horde of mosquitoes had found a buffet on the sensitive skin there. "What does this mean for us, Joann?"

Dad said, "I don't think anything would change her mind about you. She's always wanted the store and she's always wanted you. I'd hazard a guess she wants both in equal measure."

"Dad!" Joann put her hands on her hips. "Don't you think I should have a say in this?"

"Sure, sure." Dad nodded. "But Nathan, if you're waiting on a blessing from me, you have it. If you want to ask her to marry you, ask her."

"Yes, ask her," Barb said.

Joann whipped around. Barb shifted Susan in her arms as Charles looked on. This was getting out of hand. "No one here needs advice from the peanut gallery."

Barb sniffed. "Maybe you do."

Charles wore a grin to rival any jolly elf. He looked past Joann to Nathan and gave the thumbs-up.

She turned, expecting to see an embarrassed Nathan, and was about to tell her family to back off. But when she met Nathan's gaze, the world stopped. He didn't look embarrassed. He looked intense.

He was all seriousness when he said, "You did hear that I have your dad's blessing, and Barb's?"

A strange terror gripped Joann, like standing at the edge of a drop-off at the deepest, coldest part of a lake on a scorching summer day, daring yourself to dive, toes tingling in anticipation and fear.

He didn't move an inch from where he stood, but it seemed the distance between them contracted all on its own.

He said, "I completely agree with your dad's wishes. The store is your dream and I want you to have it. I'll swear an oath to honor this letter if you want me to."

"I have a stipulation."

Barb groaned, and Joann heard Charles shushing her.

Joann licked her lips. "I'll marry you if you agree to hold on to your dream as well. I'd never be happy if you gave it up for me." She touched his hair, pulled one of the brown curls straight, and then let it go. "We'll find a way."

The next thing she knew, she was deep into Nathan's kiss, forgetting how to breathe but not caring one iota. Who needed oxygen?

When Joann and Nathan finally broke apart, her family had vacated the office.

Her hands flew to her cheeks. "I can't believe we made out in front of my dad."

"Do you think he'll fire me?"

"Probably. But first he'll make you finish putting up the Christmas lights."

CHAPTER TWENTY-SIX

Joann wasn't used to her engagement ring yet. Elbow deep in bread dough, she suddenly remembered her ring and wriggled it off her finger, placing it in the holder on the kitchen windowsill. Joann smiled. The ring had been an early Christmas gift, given in private.

"How can I help?" Barb tied on a blue-striped apron.

Barb and Susan had spent the night in Barb's old room, staying over to help Joann with the meal prep. Charles would get off in time for lunch, though Christmas dinner might be served at three rather than noon.

"I've almost got it." Joann pinched off a handful of dough and rolled it in flour. "Hand me a pan, would you?"

Barb retrieved the pan from the counter and placed it on the table. One by one, Joann prepared balls of dough.

She said, "Boil water in the percolator. I need a dish of hot water to set in the oven under these rolls. The moist heat will help them rise."

Barb did as told, plugging in the appliance. "By the way, where's the cookbook?"

"Never you mind. Can you go find the cloth napkins? And put the white tapers on the table."

Trust Barb to ask about the cookbook today, of all days. All this time, she hadn't mentioned *Mrs. Canfield's Cookery Book* once. Joann had decided to wait and surprise Barb with it at Christmas. The wrapped book nestled among the other presents under the tree.

She hoped Barb liked the notes she'd added in. Second thoughts about the sappiness of her gesture set

Joann's insides quivering, but it was too late to change anything now.

The girls carried on with the meal prep.

Charles arrived, triggering Dad to share loud Christmas cheer, waking Susan. By the time Barb excused herself to tend the baby, Charles had already quieted Susie. For a moment, Joann and Barb watched the two men playing with the baby.

Barb whispered, "Two months old and she's got them both wrapped around her little finger."

Joann bumped Barb with her hip. "Takes after her mama."

Faking offense, Barb let her mouth drop open and gave Joann a gentle shove.

Joann said, "You're training her right, I think."

Barb threaded her arm through Joann's. "Let's finish up the kitchen work while we have a minute. She'll need me soon enough."

Nathan came for dinner, bringing Mr. Poole. Joann ushered the older man into the living room.

"Sit here." She gestured to Dad's La-Z-Boy.

"Oh, no ma'am." Mr. Poole tucked his chin. "I can't sit in another man's La-Z-Boy."

Dad gripped the reluctant man's shoulder. "Of course you can."

Carefully, Mr. Poole perched on the chair, as uncomfortable as a rooster in the wrong coop.

Nathan caught Joann's hand and gave it a gentle squeeze. At the rightness of it, her heart fluttered and expanded. She might explode with happiness.

Dad said, "Since dinner's running late, why don't you girls pass around the presents?"

Reluctantly, Joann loosened her grip, but Nathan wouldn't let go.

"I'll help you. We can do it together."

Earlier in the week he'd brought over a tree. The top of it cleared the ceiling by mere inches, and Dad had directed Nathan to string masses of silver foil icicles from top to bottom.

Later, Joann spread them evenly to fill in the bare patches.

The cookbook was among the last of the gifts. Barb unwrapped it, a puzzled expression coming over her face. She wore a half smile. "What's this?"

Joann said, "I'll show you."

She sat beside Barb and flipped through the pages, pausing at her writing.

"When I noticed the notes written in the cookbook, I asked Charles if I could add some of my own for you."

"This is so sweet, Jo. I love it. It's perfect." Barb crushed Joann in a tight hug.

Refusing to give way to tears, Joann quipped, "Now when you're cooking, no matter where you go, you'll have my voice in your head telling you not to burn the food."

The men chuckled. Barb wrinkled her nose at Joann before kissing her on the cheek.

"It's partly from Charles, as well." Joann turned to Charles. "Thank you for letting me add to the book. I sure hope your mother doesn't mind."

"Why would she mind?"

"I was so nervous about handling it. It is her cookbook, after all. It's so old. It must be special to her."

"I think you misunderstood. My mother collects old cookbooks, but I hadn't given this one to her yet. I got it at a bookstore meaning it for her, but when Barb said something about cooking, I gave it to her instead. I got Mom another one."

Barb's mouth dropped open. Joann and Barb gaped at each other in stunned disbelief.

Barb said, "But I thought it was an heirloom!"

"So did I!"

Charles shrugged. "It is now, isn't it?"

The girls stared at Charles, then at each other, before dissolving into laughter.

Dad chuckled. "Well, girls, I guess there's been a miscommunication."

It had been a year of miscommunications and assumptions.

Because of a lack of communication, Joann had assumed Barb would always be nearby, that Nathan would never change, and that she understood Dad's motivations for discouraging her plans. She'd gotten so many things wrong. And she wasn't the only one. Her dad and Nathan had made a few assumptions of their own.

She caught Nathan's eye. "I guess we could all work a little harder on listening and asking the right questions."

Nathan gave her a knowing smile. "Sounds like a good New Year's resolution."

It did.

During the meal, Baby Susan only cried once. After, Barb disappeared upstairs with her and didn't come back down. Joann hoped her sister was napping. She seemed to take better care of herself lately, but could be so stubborn. A trait they shared, Joann wryly admitted to herself. The trick was to sort the good kind of persistence from the kind that made life unnecessarily difficult.

Joann scraped dishes and stacked them. The leftovers went into Tupperware containers destined to go home with the guests.

From behind her, Nathan's arms came around her waist. "Hey, there." He kissed her ear. "Time for a walk?"

"Sounds perfect."

Gladly, she abandoned the dishes. As they retrieved coats from the foyer, her eyes fell on the plaque.

Trust in the LORD with all thine heart; and lean not unto thine own understanding. In all thy ways acknowledge him, and he shall direct thy paths. Proverbs 3:5-6

In all thy ways.

It came back around to trust and communication. If she'd taken the time to listen instead of doggedly following the plan she thought God had for her, she may have fared better.

She determined not only would she listen and strive to communicate with her family and Nathan, but she'd also talk to God more.

And be quietly still for as long as it took to pay attention and listen.

No one knew what an uncertain future held, but one thing *was* certain. Joann would need God's guidance to face whatever came.

THE END

RECIPE PAGE

Mock Cherry Pie

¾ cup water
½ cup raisins
2 cups cranberries
1 cup of sugar
2 Tbsp. flour
1 Tbsp. butter

Pastry for double piecrust
In a saucepan, combine the raisins with the water. Soak for twenty minutes. Add cranberries and sugar and cook over medium heat, stirring constantly until cranberries pop. Sprinkle in flour and continue stirring until mixture thickens. Add butter. Stir well. Pour into prepared pie shell. Top with lattice crust.

Bake for about thirty to forty minutes at 350° until nicely browned.

Joann

Dear Reader,

Thank you for spending time in Pecan Grove! I hope you enjoyed reading Joann's story as much as I enjoyed writing it!

All my best,

Donna Jo

Customer reviews help indie authors get noticed and allow them to continue sharing their stories. Readers can leave a review on Amazon or any of their preferred platforms.

About the Author

Life is messy and beautiful. In everyone's story, there is truth and hope. Donna Jo Stone's novels are about common struggles and finding the faith to carry on through those battles. She writes for readers of historical fiction and contemporary fiction, for both the adult and young adult market.

When she's not writing, she loves to read and talk about books, poke around in old bookshops and museums, and spend time with her family.

She is an unofficial advocate for people who are on the autism spectrum, serving primarily young adults seeking counsel about job training, parents navigating the complicated terrain of helping their child on the spectrum, and as a resource for those interested in homeschooling or afterschooling their ASD child. Her upcoming young adult book series, *Wishes and Dreams,* feature or include characters on the autism spectrum.

Get Donna Jo's newsletter to keep up with the latest news about upcoming releases and book events.

https://donnajostone.com

Novel Preview

More Historical Fiction from Donna Jo Stone

Preview from the 1970's Southern Historical Novel, *When the Wildflowers Bloom Again.*

When the Wildflowers Bloom Again

In the summer of '78, Mary Parker spends most of her time with her cousin, Sharon, listening to the BeeGees, talking about boys, and biking the rural roads of Pleasant Waters, Louisiana. Caring for her emotionally fragile mother is Mary's only worry, until one day Sharon's older half-brother finds Mary alone at the neighborhood swimming hole and takes her into the woods.

Mary can't speak of what happened next. The truth will destroy her family and cost her the relationships most precious to her.

But secrets have a way of making themselves known, and when Mary finds herself pregnant, she's forced to grapple with hard decisions. Babies are a gift from God. Mary knows this full well, but she doesn't know how to deal with a pregnancy, or who to turn to for help.

Excerpt

CHAPTER ONE

Pleasant Waters, North Louisiana, 1978

Sometimes I wished my momma understood me more, but sometimes I was glad she didn't. Caught between childhood and becoming a woman, I needed my secrets, such as they were. Or that's what I thought.

Secrets can be terrible things, something I'd come to find out before the end of my fourteenth summer.

I eased the back door open and slipped out. The crickets sang loud, and honeysuckle, heavy with scent, smelled sweeter than ever before. Underneath it all, I could almost catch a whisper calling me out into the moonlight.

Barefoot, heart thumping like a wild drum beat, I crept across the yard. Grass tickled my legs. My bike leaned into the shadows of the porch. I could've ridden it to the pond, but I left it, let the green and blue striped banana seat take on darkness.

Near the edge of the tree line, the night opened her arms and took me in, diminishing me but at the same time somehow making me bigger.

I passed the big oak tree. Even if someone happened to look out from the highest window of our two-story yellow frame house, they wouldn't see me.

In the privacy of the woods, I unbraided my long, black-brown hair. Crinkled waves fell to my waist. I lifted summer-tanned arms to the sky and spun in a slow circle. My hair was outdated, not layered like my cousin Sharon's, but it suited me.

It could be my real mother had been a flower child.

Joann

Going into the woods alone at night felt deliciously forbidden, even though I'd never been told not to wander outside when everyone slept. But still, why not? I was old enough to make up my own mind.

The dirt path was soft and fine on the soles of my feet. Time had worn away everything but the ground.

A willow tree leaned over the bank of the pond, and jasmine twisted around the tree trunk, winding its way into the branches of nearby shrubs, creating a fragrant cave. It was my secret place.

I stripped off my clothes and dropped them. The idea of snakes or other creepy crawlies made me shiver and hurry to the water's edge.

Wearing nothing but skin, I slipped into the pond, where the warm softness slid across all of me like silk.

This place was different at night. I was different.

My too-long legs and skinny arms moved easy, smoothly, and I could forget that my looks didn't match up with my parents or anyone else in the family. Momma and Daddy told me I belonged in every way that mattered, but with my ruddy skin and dark hair it was plain as plain could be I wasn't their natural-born child. Why my mother had named me Marigold was beyond me.

I went by Mary.

Out in the midnight woods, it didn't matter who I was or wasn't, because I just was. The air was bigger here, and it welcomed me. I was a part of something that could never be snatched away. I lay back and let my hair float out around my head. It probably looked romantic.

Magic lived in the woods. I could be a water nymph.

I dove, then surfaced and watched the ripples until the tiny waves disappeared into the darkness. What would it be like to be wanted? I lifted my chin and arched my neck, stretched out an arm toward the sky, imagining a mysterious someone watched me as moonlight kissed my shoulders.

The low hum of small night creatures filled the air, a serenade.

How long I floated in my own world, I didn't know. Sleep tugged at me, and I swam to my bower and got out. My hair dripped. I tipped my head to the side to gather it up, and squeezed out water. Moisture beaded on my arms and legs, my belly, and I wiped the droplets off with my hands. I put on my oversized pink T-shirt and shorts.

Once on the path back toward home, I was plain Mary again, a tired girl with damp, dirt-caked feet. Mosquitoes buzzed around my head and lit on any available flesh they could find. I slapped at them as fresh bug bites multiplied on my scabby legs and arms. I'd need calamine.

As I drew close to the house, I looked up and my heart stuttered. Every window blazed with light. I stumbled into the rough bark of a pine. The muscles in my calves twitched, eager to run back into the woods and hide, but the sight of Momma pulled at me like an unwound cord, as strong as it was invisible. She walked the porch, arms crossed over her plump middle as she gripped her elbows with work-worn hands. House robe flapping open, she shuffled into the circle cast by the porch light.

I hadn't meant to cause her worry.

My feet longed to run to her, but I caught sight of Daddy sitting on the porch swing. And he saw me. Letting out a shuddering breath, he pressed clasped hands to his lips. Deep lines bracketed his mouth. He closed his eyes tight and harsh wrinkles radiated from their corners, different without his smile. Bereft.

I wanted to slink back into the woods.

A second later, he leapt up. Four giant strides brought him to the top of the steps, where he planted his feet and glared at the woods past my shoulder. I'd done it now. Carl Parker had a kind soul, but was not a man to be trifled with. It must've been a while since they'd noticed my empty bed, because Daddy was fully dressed, wearing jeans and boots.

Had he looked for me? Had he *seen* me? I sucked in a ragged breath. A horde of baby grass snakes squirmed in the pit of my belly.

No. If he'd seen me, he would've called my name.

I shouldn't have gone out.

Hair unbound, the gray strands in her dark waves exposed and shimmering in the porch light, Momma swayed back and forth as she walked, her eyes shut, mouth moving. She was praying.

I struggled to swallow against the parchment dryness overtaking my usually ready tongue.

Daddy kept his focus on me as he said my momma's name. "Dove." He spoke so quiet the crickets might've drowned him out if they hadn't stopped singing. "She's home."

Momma opened her eyes and her tense posture eased. She took two quick steps towards me, but Daddy put out a hand, touching her on the arm.

"Don't fuss, Dove." Weariness colored his tone.

The heavy weight of his disappointment rolled across the lawn and crawled up onto my back, digging in.

What had possessed me to go out into the woods alone in the middle of the night?

My throat ached as if I'd sang a song too loud, too long.

He drew a deep breath and exhaled slowly. "It appears Mary is fine." He scrubbed the chin stubble peppering his jaw and then cleared his throat. "But I believe she needs to explain herself."

Momma dropped her hands to her sides and hid them in the fabric of her robe.

She'd been reaching for me.

At first, I lurched towards her, then caught myself. I wasn't a baby anymore, running to Momma. I bent my head down and studied the mud caked between my toes before glancing back up. Momma came around Daddy and sat on the step. With a face as placid and unreadable as the summer moon, she waited to hear him out. To hear me out.

I sucked on my bottom lip, unable to express a yearning I didn't understand myself. The night had called me, but that sounded stupid in the blaze of the porch light.

"Explain!" Daddy's bark made me jump.

"I couldn't sleep," I blurted out. "So I walked to the pond."

"You've been gone a long time." Daddy crossed his arms. "Where else did you go?"

"Nowhere."

He'd moved, and in the porch light his face was all shadows and gargoyle lines. "It doesn't take three hours to walk to the pond."

I said nothing.

Daddy raked a hand through his short, dark hair. "What were you doing there?"

The bite in his tone snuffed out my guilt. He acted as if I'd committed the crime of the century. Why couldn't it be like it used to be when he took me fishing? We used to go out there at night all the time.

Momma sat patiently on the step, blinking in her mild way.

I stilled my fidgeting and chewed the inside of my cheek. I hadn't done anything awful. Just needed a taste of freedom away from the smothering house and its lonely corners that hemmed me in.

Quiet as Momma, I said, "I went swimming. That's all."

"That's not all. I expect you to have better sense. Look at your mother."

I did look, and felt bad. She was gray around the edges, but I'd been fine. I didn't need to be worried over so much. But worry she would. I knew that.

Daddy pounded a nail in. "You'll be the death of her."

Momma shook her head, but Daddy carried on.

Exhaustion settled over me as he droned on, a mosquito buzzing. Pretty soon, he'd get tired of repeating himself. I wished he'd hurry so we could go in. Now that my adventure was over, I needed sleep, and the toilet.

Pausing, Daddy cocked his head to the side and looked me over as if seeing me clear for the first time.

My heart rolled over with a thump.

He said, "Where's your bathing suit?"

Heat poured up my neck and shame pitchfork-pricked my cheeks. The throat dryness was back, and it took me a minute to respond. "I didn't wear one."

Daddy's face mottled purple-red. "You were out in the woods doing who-knows-what with who-knows-who *naked*?"

Momma sprang to her feet and tugged at his sleeve, talking low with her mouth close to his ear, but he kept on shouting.

"Were there boys?" His voice echoed beyond the pool of light cast by the porch and house, loud enough to travel through the surrounding trees and to the neighbors'. If he didn't hush, tongues would wag tomorrow.

"No, Daddy!" I whisper-yelled, my clenched together fists hidden behind my back.

"Carl!" Momma clasped her throat.

Boots clomping loud, Daddy paced and muttered under his breath.

Momma flew down the steps toward me and stopped an arm's length away, waiting, expectant.

A good daughter wouldn't have run into the woods without a thought. I couldn't give her what she wanted, because I didn't know how to be that girl. Instead, I doubled down and kept my peace.

"Mary, why did you sneak out?" A bit of steel glinted in her soft, gray eyes, but her gentle voice was as calm as the pond had been before I'd splashed my way in. "What's bothering you?"

I turned away a fraction. I didn't want to have a heart to heart, and I hated her for trying so hard, then hated myself for possessing such a thought.

What was wrong with me?

My lungs ached for air and space.

"I wanted to. That's all." Itchy to get away and regretting the ruined night, I said, "I'm sorry for worrying you."

I think I meant it.

"Look at me." My gaze met hers. "Is there anything you want to tell me?"

"No, Momma." I poked a finger into the hem of my shirt and twisted until my circulation almost cut off. "I felt restless and went for a swim, that's all." The last speck of resistance dribbled out of me. I hung my head. "I'm sorry." From under my lashes, I stole a glance at Daddy.

Deep frown lines gouged creases into his forehead. Momma would calm him down. Anyway, by morning he wouldn't be mad at me anymore.

Momma kept her gaze pinned on Daddy's when she asked me, "Was anyone else there?"

I put my shoulders back and lifted my chin. "No. I was alone."

Joann

It was the truth, and Momma believed me.

What she didn't know was that I hadn't *wanted* to be alone.

Acknowledgements

I couldn't have finished the work without support and help.

Thanks to Jenny for inviting me to join the project, and the apron strings authors for propping me up with their prayers. Special thanks to Samantha Fury, who designed the covers for our series and suffered through endless messages with grace and patience until we got the cover just right.

Sending a shout out to my amazing beta readers. Jayna Morrow not only took time out of her busy schedule to point out developmental issues, but tracked down errant commas and put them in the correct places. Sandy Bruney's wisdom and experience has been a great blessing. Felicia Bridges willingness to share her knowledge was a tremendous help. You guys are the bomb.

Thanks to my Thursday crew, Carrie Walker, beta reader and critique partner, Andra Loy, who always helps me see the lighter side of things, and Stephanie Daniels, who can brighten any day. And all three for their steadfast friendship, even when I whine about how hard writing is. It is very hard. Harder than I ever thought it would be. I'm so glad I have you guys to hang out with every week.

P.J. Leigh's constant encouragement is a true blessing. Thank you for checking in on me, reading my manuscripts, and cheering me on.

Thank you to my loves for being there. And to my readers, thank you for reading and supporting my dream! Above all else, I am gratefully thankful to the One who makes it all possible.